'I was nuts about you.'

Francesca told him crossly, 'If I so much as glimpsed you it made my day.'

'Yeah? You never spoke to me unless I asked you a direct question, and then you squeaked out the minimum you could get away with,' Luke challenged. 'You always acted as if you were terrified of me.'

'Yes! Yes, I did! Because I thought you were so wonderful that it just froze me up. Don't you know *anything* about well-sheltered teenage girls, Luke?'

After living in the USA for nearly eight years, **Lilian Darcy** is back in her native Australia with her American historian husband and their three young children. More than ever, writing is a treat for her now, looked forward to and luxuriated in like a hot bath after a hard day. She likes to create modern heroes and heroines with good doses of zest and humour in their make-up, and relishes the opportunity that the medical series gives her for dealing with genuine, gripping drama in romance and in daily life. She finds research fascinating too—everything from attacking learned medical tomes to spending a day in a maternity ward.

Recent titles by the same author:

MAKING BABIES
INCURABLY ISABELLE
A SPECIALIST'S OPINION
MISLEADING SYMPTOMS

WANTING
DR WILDE

BY
LILIAN DARCY

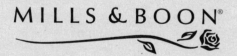

DID YOU PURCHASE THIS BOOK WITHOUT A COVER?

If you did, you should be aware it is **stolen property** as it was reported *unsold* and *destroyed* by a retailer. Neither the author nor the publisher has received any payment for this book.

All the characters in this book have no existence outside the imagination of the author, and have no relation whatsoever to anyone bearing the same name or names. They are not even distantly inspired by any individual known or unknown to the author, and all the incidents are pure invention.

All Rights Reserved including the right of reproduction in whole or in part in any form. This edition is published by arrangement with Harlequin Enterprises II B.V. The text of this publication or any part thereof may not be reproduced or transmitted in any form or by any means, electronic or mechanical, including photocopying, recording, storage in an information retrieval system, or otherwise, without the written permission of the publisher.

This book is sold subject to the condition that it shall not, by way of trade or otherwise, be lent, resold, hired out or otherwise circulated without the prior consent of the publisher in any form of binding or cover other than that in which it is published and without a similar condition including this condition being imposed on the subsequent purchaser.

MILLS & BOON and MILLS & BOON with the Rose Device are registered trademarks of the publisher.

*First published in Great Britain 1998
Harlequin Mills & Boon Limited,
Eton House, 18-24 Paradise Road, Richmond, Surrey TW9 1SR*

© Lilian Darcy 1998

ISBN 0 263 80799 1

*Set in Times Roman 10 on 11¼ pt.
03-9806-56204-D*

*Printed and bound in Great Britain
by Mackays of Chatham PLC, Chatham*

CHAPTER ONE

'YOU'LL be meeting ghosts around every corner,' locum Dr Preston Stock laughed.

'Ghosts?' Francesca Brady was startled.

'Of your former self,' he clarified. 'I hadn't realised you grew up in this town.'

'Yes, but I left at eighteen,' she said a little defensively, 'and I'm thirty now. Twelve years with barely even a vacation visit, as my parents usually came down to see me or we went to Florida. I very much doubt there'll be ghosts.'

'Ah, but that's exactly when there are ghosts.' He wagged a well-manicured finger. 'When you *haven't* been back. There's been no chance for you to overlay the past with more recent, less confronting memories.'

'You sound as if you think my past has been particularly lurid, Dr Stock,' she grumbled.

He evidently considered this debriefing lunch his rightful opportunity to make wise pronouncements on a whole range of topics. He'd already verbally slaughtered Darrensberg's social scene, its shopping opportunities and many of its citizens. Now he was starting on her!

'Darling,' he drawled, '*Everyone* has a lurid past.'

'*I* don't,' she said haughtily. 'I have a very nice past. A stable, caring mother, a father who was successful and respected in his profession, an older brother and sister I got on well with. In short, a very happy childhood. There'll be no ghosts.'

'If you say so,' he replied kindly.

They were silent for a moment as they each made inroads into the main course of their meal. Francesca had decided to treat Dr Stock to lunch in Darrensberg's best restaurant as a parting gesture, but she was beginning to feel he didn't deserve it. The man had gossiped about everything under the sun, but had said almost nothing about the family practice which he had run for three months and which she was about to take over. Why had Dad chosen him? It worried her a little.

She decided to bring their discussion back to business in no uncertain terms, and began briskly, after swallowing a delectable mouthful of salmon ravioli in caviar cream sauce, 'Now, Dad's heart attack came at the end of February and you took over the practice almost straight away. In a minute I'd like you to give me a run-down on the patients you think I should hear about from you personally but, first, were you aware of losing any patients after Dad's retirement? Did anyone express any dissatisfaction at the change?

'After all, it was so sudden, and—evidently you didn't realise this—Dad was here for nearly forty years. You did make it clear from the start, didn't you, that I'd be taking up the reins permanently as soon as my family practice residency in New Jersey finished?'

'I did, yes,' Preston answered. 'God, I can't imagine *anyone* could have thought that I was planning to stay here for ever! As far as dissatisfaction, or any losing of patients, not that I'm aware of. Patients you should hear about personally? When we head back I'll run through Mrs Mayberry's appointment book to remind me of the cases that'll make you reach for the headache pills and I'll give you the low-down, although there are a couple I can think of *straight* off the top of my head!

'Anyway, and, yes, I did tell everyone that Frank Brady's daughter would be taking over in June, but it didn't bring much comment, actually. That's why I concluded your father must have come to practise here once you'd already left home. Evidently you were a bit of a goody two-shoes and didn't leave much of an impression on the Darrensberg collective consciousness.'

'I was *not* a goody two-shoes!' Really, this man was impossible! 'I was—somewhat shy, that's all, and the youngest child.'

Inwardly, though, she had to admit that Preston Stock had a point. In addition to her undoubted shyness, she *had* been a dreadful goody two-shoes as a child, and even a teenager—always doing exactly as she was told, always neatly dressed with her blonde hair tied back, always up to date with homework and never creating a breath of scandal.

She shuddered, and was a little amused, at the memory.

And as for 'the Darrensberg collective consciousness', she certainly intended to make an impression upon it now.

'As to losing patients because of the transition,' Preston Stock was saying. 'Unlikely. Where else are they going to go? Drive to Wayans Falls? Oh, I mean, there's Dr Wilde, of course, but so far he doesn't seem like much competition. People haven't got a good word to say about the guy.'

'Dr Wilde?' she was astonished. 'But surely he can't still be practising! He lost his licence years ago. Or at least…' She frowned.

Dad had kept her up to date with what was happening in the small medical world of Darrensberg and nearby towns but, to be honest, she hadn't always taken it all in. She remembered, in particular, a couple of her parents' visits to New York around exam time when all she'd been able to think of was how to keep her eyes open long enough to finish her dinner.

Medical malpractice in a small rural town had seemed like a mere tempest in a teapot, compared to failing finals, since at that stage, years before Dad's illness, she hadn't considered the possibility of returning to Darrensberg.

She continued, less certainly, 'At the very least he must be retired, I'd have thought. He was older than Dad!'

'Old? Not *this* Dr Wilde, darling.' Dr Stock grinned. 'Must be the son of your guy, I guess.'

'The son? Adam,' she concluded. 'OK, Adam has taken over his father's practice.'

She was a little surprised. Dad hadn't mentioned it. What *had* Dad said? His voice had been so frighteningly weak as he lay in his hospital bed in New York after the heart attack which had nearly claimed his life during a weekend visit to the city. At that stage, not yet having accepted what the state of his health would do to his future, he had still been talking of returning to practice within a few weeks.

It had only been her promise to take over the Brady Family Practice Center herself which had finally brought him to see sense on the issue of retirement. Even after that, Francesca and her mother had had to conspire together to stop him from fretting and obsessing over his practice, which now left her with the uncomfortable feeling that she didn't know quite as much about the situation in Darrensberg as she should. Witness this revelation that Adam Wilde had now set up in practice here.

'I'd thought he was headed for a law career,' she murmured. He had left for college in Boston when she was eleven, well before the apparent degeneration in his father's practice.

'No, not *Adam* Wilde,' Dr Stock was saying. 'His name's Luke.'

'*Luke*? Luke Wilde? A doctor? That's...' She laughed, completely incredulous now. If Adam Wilde as a doctor here was surprising, then Luke was... 'Impossible. Luke was... He was...' She trailed off, remembering very clearly exactly what Luke Wilde had been fifteen years ago.

Preston studied her, then laughed. 'There you are! What did I tell you? Ghosts! Powerful ones, too, judging by the expression on your face.'

'It's not ghosts,' she said crisply. 'No one has died. I'm just...astounded, that's all. Luke Wilde dropped out of school. He rode a Harley-Davidson, and there were rumours about drugs. He ran with a bad crowd. I can't believe he's a doctor now!'

'"Ran with a bad crowd",' Preston Stock mimicked lightly. 'Gee, you really were a goody two-shoes, weren't you?'

This time she didn't bother to deny it. She didn't, in fact, say anything at all. She was far too busy thinking about Luke Wilde, and the ghosts Preston had teased her with were crowding into her mind like a thick flock of birds.

Luke.

She'd had the most *horrible* crush on him! Or was 'wonderful' a better word? Oh, God, it had gone on for years! She had been thirteen when it started, while he was seventeen and already in trouble, and it hadn't ended until...

Thinking back, if she was honest it hadn't ended until she'd left for college in New York at eighteen, though Luke himself had been long gone at that stage, and her aching, blissful infatuation had been nourished purely by two years of memories. The sight of him roaring past on his bike, his sultry presence on their back porch as he hung out on summer nights—much to her parents' disapproval—with her older brother Chris and, most powerfully, the one incandescent evening when he had kissed her.

Oh, thank goodness you grew out of that sort of thing! Dreaming about him at night, obsessively analysing every meaningless, casual word he happened to say to her, sitting on the front steps for *hours* pretending to read in the vain hope that he'd cruise past.

If he had cruised past or—miracle of miracles—stopped by to see Chris and actually condescended to speak to her, she'd been so churned up she'd been unable to eat dinner that night, and she wouldn't even have heard what had been said to her over the meal because she'd been so busy with her fifteen-year-old fantasies of taming his wicked ways with the power of her love—even though, she decided cynically now, his wicked ways must surely have been a good part of the attraction—and then marrying him in a blaze of glory and white tulle and riding off into the sunset with him on the back of that evil black bike.

She smiled down at her dwindling plate of ravioli. Yes, thank goodness you grew out of it!

She couldn't even remember his face now, just had a hazy image of his young, strong, leather-clad male body and a pair of angry blue eyes. He'd served a purpose, though, she supposed in a clinical sort of way. Her fantasies about him had safely channelled her burgeoning hormones while at the same time filling her with a desire to *prove* herself to him—make him notice her.

As she had been, quite definitely, the most horrible goody two-shoes Darrensberg had ever produced, this proving herself had taken the form of studying hard and obtaining outstanding results at school, thus allowing her to breeze into the pre-med programme at Columbia University in New York. Luke Wilde had, to all intents and purposes, vanished by this time and had not been spoken of except in terms of darkest rumour. Hadn't he had quite a serious motorbike accident in New Jersey? He had known absolutely nothing of this feat of hers.

She had to thank him for it, though, she reflected, because now she was very nicely qualified as a specialist in family practice…but, then, incredible though it seemed, evidently he was too.

She still couldn't quite believe it. What was Luke Wilde like now, fifteen years since they'd last met? Her imagination utterly refused to produce a credible picture.

'As for those patients I mentioned, there are a couple of real horrors,' Preston Stock was saying, and Francesca realised guiltily that he'd been doing exactly as she had asked him to do and was giving her a run-down on patients, of which she had thus far heard not a single word, though presumably she must have been giving enough polite nods to encourage him to keep going.

Now, belatedly, she focused. 'Yes? Like who?'

'Well, first and foremost, of course, there's Sharon Baron,' Preston said.

'*Who*?'

'Sharon Baron. Her parents evidently believed that a witty name is a pretty name. She tells me she has a brother, Daron, and a sister, Caron, but so far I haven't had the good fortune to meet them. I meet Sharon fairly frequently, however.'

Preston proceeded to exercise his rather cruel linguistic fluency at the expense of her future patients for some fifteen minutes more, but as she'd asked for it she couldn't complain and she was still guiltily aware that her attention was not focused as thoroughly as it should be.

Sipping coffee and nibbling on a piece of caramel tart, she just couldn't get out of her mind the incongruous fact that Luke Wilde, of all people, was a *doctor*!

When Preston had finished his run-down, she jumped in immediately to say with a frown and a not entirely successful attempt to sound casual, 'You said I wouldn't have much competition because Luke…Dr Wilde is so unpopular. Wh-why is that, exactly?'

'Oh.' Preston shrugged. 'You've said it already. His wild youth. People don't forget. The rumours are rather nasty in this case, though I'm hazy on the details. And if old Dr Wilde really did lose his licence to practise—hadn't heard that one, actually. It's juicy! I wonder what he did? As for Luke's current incarnation, drugs, of course. Whenever a doctor is unpopular there are always rumours about drugs—feeding his addiction by writing fake prescriptions, shooting up between patients—you know the sort of thing. Perhaps in this case it's true.'

'I—I doubt it,' she answered, feeling an absurd wash of disappointment, even horror, at the idea. What? After all these years would she still take it personally if he hadn't reformed, as he'd done so dashingly under her golden influence in all those silly teenage fantasies of hers?

But, no, she couldn't laugh about it. Drug-taking by a doctor was an extremely serious thing. Luke had been wild but not, *surely* not, the type who'd go on to abuse his profession in such a way.

She went on, carefully neutral, 'Perhaps you've just talked to the wrong people?'

'Perhaps…' He shrugged again. He didn't seem to care particularly if the rumour he'd so casually passed on was true or not. He added lightly, 'On the two occasions we met I didn't observe any tell-tale signs, I must say.'

'Well, I must phone or drop round fairly soon and make contact,' she mused aloud. 'There was something of a rivalry between Dad and old Dr Wilde twenty years ago, but that's crazy now. There's plenty of room in this town for two doctors these days. We ought to be friends…or friendly colleagues, at least. I'm sure this business about drugs…'

'Oh, no doubt! *Everything's* exaggerated in a town like this! I wouldn't like to guess what they're saying about *me*!' Preston had finished his coffee now, and was shifting a little restlessly. 'And now, if you don't mind,' he continued, 'I want to head back to New York this afternoon. I start in a nice, cushy Manhattan dermatology practice on Monday—and we need to have that tour of the office.'

'Sure.' She nodded.

She could see that he was already looking ahead, brushing Darrensberg and its citizens aside. His time in the practice had given him three months' casual employment between real jobs, as well as a little rather catty amusement, but that was all.

Not that she could blame him for feeling that way. In a locum position it would be crazy to get deeply involved. Darrensberg contained her professional future, not his. And evidently it contained Luke Wilde's professional future, too. She was still curious, still found it hard to believe.

Old Dr Wilde's surgery and residence was just half a block along from the Brady practice, but the latter was closer to the centre of town so Francesca and Preston didn't pass by Dr Wilde's as they walked back from the restaurant. The Wildes' large Victorian house was set back a little from the road, too, so her covert glance up the street yielded no view of it.

'The one thing I do envy you,' Preston said as they went along the path down the side of the house to the surgery entrance, 'is this place. I'll be living in a one-bedroom Manhattan apartment as of tonight.'

'Yes, I've always loved it,' Francesca agreed somewhat smugly.

Like the Wildes' house, it was an imposing mansion, dating from the days last century when logging in the magnificent forests of the surrounding Adirondack mountains had made the town prosperous. These days Darrensberg was less prosperous, though still very much a living town, and its money came far more from tourism—skiing in winter at the nearby resort of Eagle Mountain, with watersports and wilderness pursuits in summer along the Hudson River and in and around the region's many lakes.

Most of the Victorian dwellings remained. Some had been revamped as bed-and-breakfast inns and a restaurant or two, such as the Gables where they had just eaten, others continued as professional rooms such as the Brady Family Practice Center, and a few, sadly, were on the point of collapse and decay.

Of all these places, the Brady house was Francesca's favourite, partly just because it was home, of course, but also because her parents had taken such good care of it over the years.

Last fall, before Dad's heart attack, he had had the whole place repainted inside and out in the latest designer colours, had updated the furnace, completely remodelled the kitchen, had the hardwood floors resanded, and repaired a couple of weak spots in the beautiful slate roof. Apparently, it hadn't been a trouble-free process, either. The first kitchen contractor had gone broke and never completed some of the work he had been paid for. Dad had then felt the need to supervise the second contractor with meticulous care.

'Which was too much for him to have to worry over,' Mrs Brady had said to Francesca one day when Dr Brady was still in hospital. 'Perhaps if he hadn't had all that stress and strain his heart would have held up. And he just can't *delegate*, you see. You know what he's like! He can't believe that anyone else is either competent or honest, and when something like this happens with that horrible kitchen man to prove him right…!'

Shaking hands had spread helplessly, alarming Francesca about her mother's state of health as well as her father's.

'*Don't* let him meddle in the practice any more, Francesca,' Mrs Brady had finished beseechingly. 'If he starts to talk about it just cut him off. Tell him I've told you whatever it is already. *Remind* him that you're more qualified than he is now!'

She'd had to do it, too! There had been lots of interfering phone calls from Florida to deflect over the past few months since her parents had taken up permanent residence in their vacation condominium. It had been a difficult time, and Dr Stock's less than alluring personality was a tribute to the fact that her father's decisions had been made under the worst circumstances.

I should have insisted on arranging the locum appointment myself! she realised now, pointlessly.

She and Preston reached the waiting-room entrance at the same time and had a small silent tussle of body language over who was ushering whom inside. Francesca won, and it seemed significant. This was the point at which she quite definitely took over!

Preston flipped through the appointment book and re-membered several more patients she needed to hear about, updated her on the contents of the dispensary, as well as the relative merits of the various pharmaceutical reps who called on an intermittent basis, and outlined the schedule of surgery hours that he'd kept. In this it seemed he had been content to follow her father's procedure very exactly, but she planned to review all that and make changes. She wanted to assert her identity, to impose her own stamp on the practice now.

Then Preston said, 'Here are the keys. You probably re-member them and what they unlock. Those childhood things come back fast.'

'Like the ghosts?' she couldn't help saying.

'Like the ghosts,' he agreed blandly. 'Now, you have my New York address and phone number if there's anything else needs winding up. Mind if I head off now?'

'Fine. As you said, I can call you if I need to, and I have unpacking to do myself.'

She had only arrived that morning, having sent her bulk-ier possessions on ahead yesterday and brought the more personal items with her in the car.

Preston Stock gave a last rather knowing goodbye, and drawled, 'Keep in touch.' It was as if he fully expected more than one panicky phone call over the next couple of weeks.

Then he was gone, leaving her to face the silence of this big place and the sight of her things piled in the hall and the big Victorian kitchen.

She ought to get straight to it. Ought to, but didn't. She felt rather restless, and wandered around for a good half hour, admiring the new paintwork, rediscovering familiar rooms, noting the furnishings her parents had left—her mother, really, since she had had to handle almost all of this work—and those they'd taken with them to the Florida condo.

Preston had conducted a final series of office appointments this morning and she wasn't seeing patients herself until Monday so she had a bit of time before unpacking became imperative, and it suddenly occurred to her that Luke Wilde might be home.

She could go and see him. Right now. She could re-introduce herself. Assess the man as he now was and hopefully scotch any reason to believe Preston's unattractively gossipy tales. She would bury the hatchet of the old Wilde-Brady professional rivalry, which struck her as rather amusingly small-town now, and start to forge a positive and productive link with her new colleague—and old heart-throb.

She smiled at that thought, feeling the strength of her new position here and an indulgent fondness for her shy, prim old self and the unexpectedly passionate fantasy life she'd had back then. Luke would have laughed aloud if he'd known! She'd have died a thousand deaths of embarrassment to have her tender dreams exposed to his wickedly cynical scrutiny. What on earth was he going to be like now?

There was one way to find out. Locking the house again, she set off down the street, which was basking in the mild afternoon sunshine of late May. People were mowing their lawns—possibly for the first time since winter—and the air was filled with the buzz of power mowers and the pleasant scent of fresh-mown grass. Perhaps Luke would be mowing his lawn, too.

The image was a very domestic one, and it occurred to her that he might well be married. With children even. He'd be thirty-four now. Suddenly her impulsive errand seemed a little more confronting, a little more fraught with the possibility of disaster, and she *still* couldn't form a plausible picture of the man.

Perhaps it was a mistake to be doing this. What was the true substance behind her father's cryptic complaints about old Dr Wilde's practice and all his predictions of doom? On the few occasions when she'd asked for real details Dad had dismissed the matter, telling her 'not to worry her head with it'. She wondered when Luke Wilde had taken over. Dad hadn't mentioned it. It was possible that he didn't even know. Perhaps doing this *was* a mistake.

To chicken out now, though, would remind her a little too strongly of the fifteen-year-old she had been when they'd last met so she kept going, as outwardly confident as when she had started.

Then, a hundred yards along, the Wilde house came into view, and it was her second major shock of the day.

At first she just couldn't believe it. Maybe she'd remembered wrongly, and this was the Keating place next door. But, no, the layout of the house was right, and its setting some yards from the property's frontage looked familiar. All the details, though...

The wraparound porch was sagging, and half its decorative wooden trim was gone. The sturdy Victorian clapboard, of which even the most magnificent old houses in this region were constructed, was peeling and ill-tended. The once lovely garden had gone to rack and ruin, she saw—although the lawn had been recently mown—and there were three cracked window-panes on the upper storeys and slates were missing from the patterned roof.

Was this the result of old Dr Wilde's scandal-laden departure from practice? In what little thought she'd given to the matter, she had never considered something like this! She hesitated. Should she go back? No, because she might have been seen from a window...

Which door to attempt, though? The imposing but shabby front entrance? Or the side door, which was, as at her place, the entrance to the waiting room, surgery and office. Then she saw that the latter door was open, which made the decision for her.

Walking up the side steps, she thought that of all the emotions she might have expected a meeting with Luke Wilde to arouse in her after so long, this was one she absolutely hadn't considered—pity.

There was no one in the shabby waiting room, but there was a bell on the rather nice antique front desk and a neatly printed sign, reading, PLEASE RING AND SIT DOWN.

She hesitated and wished intensely that she'd done the sensible thing and phoned first—or taken more notice of the way Preston Stock had dismissed the resurrected Wilde practice as irrelevant and a failure, and questioned him more closely about those rumours. Who had he heard them from? What was the evidence? And how long since Luke had taken over here? If she had realised things were this bad she'd never have just dropped in like this.

Should she ring that bell? She listened, motionless. Everything was very quiet. Perhaps, if no one was about, she could just noiselessly let herself out and flee back down the street again.

Yes, that would be much the best thing to do. She started to tiptoe back towards the door, but a tell-tale Victorian hardwood floorboard creaked beneath her feet, she heard a movement from the office, a drawer closing and a sound that she subconsciously recognised but didn't have time to identify. A moment later, while her back was still turned, there came a male voice, saying with gravelly politeness, 'Can I help you?'

Her heart plummeting, she turned, feeling like a thief caught in the act, and faced him, mute with the shock of mingled recognition and discovery.

Yes, it was definitely Luke Wilde, staring at her as he completed the fastening of a shirt cuff. Luke, the man who had single-handedly robbed her of dozens of hours of teenage sleep.

He looked at her blankly for a timeless moment while she searched desperately for the right thing to say, then that gravelly voice sounded again, with an added rasp in it this time as he said disbelievingly, 'Chess? Chess *Brady*?'

CHAPTER TWO

'CHESS.'

No one had called Francesca that in years. Even her brother, Chris, who had originated the nickname, didn't use it now, but of course he *had* used it fifteen years ago—all the time—and so that was how Luke Wilde thought of her.

'I'm amazed that you recognised me,' she managed.

'Oh, yes,' he replied lightly, 'I recognised you. Took a second or two—time stood still, as they say.' His smile was twisted and cynical. 'But, really, you haven't changed much. Still a pretty blonde princess.'

It was so deliberately dismissive that she gasped in shock and felt the burn of anger colouring her cheeks.

'I'm a little more than that, I think.' Formally, she held out her hand to him. 'Dr Francesca Brady now, taking over my father's practice.'

'I know,' he nodded briefly. 'When do you start?'

'Monday.'

'I'd heard, of course, but I hadn't realised it was so soon.'

He hadn't taken her hand, but she was damned if she'd let him win with *that* little bit of power play! She wasn't fifteen any more, and crippled by a crush. She kept her hand out and met his gaze—still blue, still angry—full on with her own grey eyes, and after another moment, with cold reluctance, he stretched his hand out too and their palms met in a formal clasp.

There was memory and electricity in his touch, ambushing her out of nowhere and taking her completely by surprise. Hell, she *wasn't* fifteen to be set on fire by the touch of a man's hand! Was *he* aware of it?

Evidently not, which was fortunate. He had removed his hand as quickly as decency allowed and was still staring at her, his blue eyes flicking down and then up again, as sneeringly dismissive in intent as his words to her had been.

Neither of them spoke. Again it was a battle of wills and it gave her time to make a rough and still incredulous inventory of the changes in him.

At some level her memory of him had been so strong that she'd still half expected to see him dressed in leather and cradling a biker's helmet beneath his arm but, of course, he wasn't. That dangerous image had been such a large part of the attraction, though, that his current conservative attire seemed unconvincing, a disguise—as much befitting his real nature as the 'court clothes' delinquent youths dressed up in around these parts to go before a judge when charged with stealing a car.

He was wearing neat, pale grey pants, textured and tailored, below a white shirt. Black leather shoes, well-polished. A *tie*, for heaven's sake! It even matched the pants, with its tones of darker grey. She dismissed the clothes. They couldn't belong to the Luke Wilde she had known.

And yet, if she really thought about it, they suited him. He looked…well, incredibly male, incredibly capable, dressed like this, the body beneath the civilised fabrics strong and tautly formed.

'I have appointment hours at the moment,' he said at last. 'Is there any particular reason you've come?'

'Oh, you have a patient with you?'

'Not right now.'

'Then…then…' She was determined to push past this horrible, hostile beginning, so utterly unexpected, but he wasn't making it easy for her and for a moment her control slipped. Deliberately, in order to get it firmly back in place, she recalled the contrast between the prosperous state of her own office and home and this run-down establishment.

Luke Wilde had absolutely no reason to feel superior to her in any way!

'I thought we ought to meet and talk,' she began again, far more briskly, then, warming to the subject, 'Our fathers never got on, I know, professionally or personally, but you and my brother, Chris, were friends. I've always had…' her voice caught slightly in her throat '…very, uh, warm memories of you, Luke, and I don't see why we shouldn't both be able to practise very successfully in Darrensberg.'

Deliberately she didn't refer to the rumours she'd heard, either past or present, and went on, brisk again, 'There's easily room for two doctors, and I expect we both have slightly different areas of special interest. We could confer occasionally, send each other patients. For example, before switching to family practice, I did a year's training in—'

'God, I don't believe this!' he cut in heavily. 'You just waltz back into town with your squeaky-clean medical degrees, inherit all Daddy's loyal paying customers, and then think we can be "friends." "Colleagues." "Exchange patients." "Confer." I won't have a bar of it, I'm sorry.'

'There *is* room for two doctors!'

'Tell your father that!'

'Dad has nothing to do with this, and I have no intention of involving him in any way.' She was furious now, too, at the sneering way Luke had brought him into the conversation—or was tirade a more accurate word? 'He had a serious heart attack four months ago.' Her throat tightened. 'And could only be persuaded to retire on the condition that I took over. Which I have! Now, I don't know the full story of…' She hesitated. It was scarcely an issue you could bring up tactfully. 'Of your father's giving up practice, but surely that's irrelevant now. I'm certainly not planning to hold it against *you*! We're the next generation, we can start again and make it work this time. I—I don't see why you're so angry.'

'No, clearly you don't.' It wasn't quite a sneer. She recoiled at his tone, and he laughed briefly. 'I'm frightening you, aren't I?'

'You could hardly do that,' she retorted. 'You overestimate yourself. You are…worrying me, though.'

'Yes, I can see that. You've gone all wide-eyed. God, I remember it from fifteen years ago! Like father, like daughter. I was always the bad boy to you, wasn't I? You could never get past that since you'd never done one bad thing in your life. Sometimes, the way you'd look at me…! As if I was about to eat you up. There were a couple of times when I was sorely tempted to—'

He stopped abruptly, way before she could possibly guess at the end of his sentence. Somehow, though, the passion behind his words had flung a memory into her mind that was complete in every detail—the time he had kissed her.

He *couldn't* have been thinking of that now! She hadn't thought of it herself in years, though she'd relived it in her thoughts and dreams for months and months afterwards until gradually its power had lessened. Now, though, that power returned in full force and, to her horror, she felt her nipples tighten into furled buds at the thought of that long, magic moment in her parents' garden.

It ought to have been funny, really. It really ought! Such a classic, clichéd list of ingredients. The brooding youth with the bad reputation and the innocent, obedient girl. The dusk-softened summer garden. The rare, unlooked-for moment alone which had taken her quite by surprise after all those months of vainly trying to engineer it.

Then his swift seizing of opportunity. It could have been clumsy, but it hadn't been. She remembered how he had looked up into the house to make sure no one was watching from the lighted windows. Then he had lunged at her with dark, fluid grace, taking her face between his palms and pulling her mouth swiftly to his as if knowing that the chance would be gone in another minute.

She had never been kissed before. Never even come close. She was barely fifteen. She had had *no idea* that it could possibly feel like that—so heady, so physical, so primitively arousing. She had gasped, frozen at first, and then had feverishly started kissing him back, stretching up because he must have been a good foot taller than she was. He was *still* a good foot taller than she was, in fact.

Then… Then… Now, this was hysterical, really! She had tried to muss up his hair, because she'd seen it done in films—God, her response to him must have been so clichéd, so inept—but he was wearing it aggressively short back then and she remembered how there hadn't been anything *to* muss, just a feathery yet slightly prickly nap of short dark strands that smelled of balsam shampoo.

Then, before it had lasted more than a few miraculous moments, they had both heard her mother's voice, sounding a little high and urgent. 'Chessie, where are you?' He'd torn his mouth from hers and vanished into the night without either of them, during the entire episode, exchanging so much as a single word.

Really, it was ridiculous. Quite laughable to think of it now.

It *should* have been ridiculous and laughable, anyway. But somehow it wasn't. Somehow it was still one of the most powerful memories of her life, right up there along with the first time she'd delivered a baby and the first time she'd witnessed a patient's death, and she had to wonder what was wrong with her now that this should be the case.

Had her life been so uneventful and lacking in drama? *Was* something wrong with her? Even at this very moment her palms were damp and she badly needed to sit down, but to do this she would have had to retreat several yards to one of the shabby black vinyl chairs set around his waiting-room walls so she had to keep standing—far too close to him for comfort.

It was, in fact, the closest she'd been to him and the only

time they'd been alone together since that memorable, long-ago night.

But it was the last thing in the world that could possibly be filling *his* thoughts.

She still wanted to sit down, and was very stubbornly determined to argue him out of this pointless hostility of his now that the first shock of it was past. She refused to be at odds with her sole professional colleague in Darrensberg! 'Look, could we have coffee or something? I'd really like to get to—'

'No, we could *not* have coffee!' he retorted. 'Despite what I've said, you still persist in thinking of our future in this town as a series of nice, cosy, supportive professional collaborations and exchanges, don't you? It's not going to happen, Francesca.' No more Chess, she noticed. 'Fifteen years ago, your naïvety was…' He hesitated, took a breath.

'Sweet,' he said. 'Now—get real, OK? I dislike and despise your father more than practically anyone else I've ever known. I won't say that feeling extends to you. I guess it doesn't.' Clearly, it was a reluctant admission. 'But I'm not exactly going to love watching your practice wax fat and prosperous while I'm working my—' He stopped and suppressed the crude expression. 'Working my little tail off,' he amended, 'to even survive. Can't you see that?'

'I— Yes, I can see that, I guess,' she conceded, still at a huge loss.

He obviously had a *b-a-ad* chip on one of those strong male shoulders of his. Just why was her father the root of all misfortune here, though? *His* father was the one who'd lost his licence due to malpractice, wasn't he? Luke had got something twisted. Suddenly she felt a little sorry for him.

Whatever it was that he'd got wrong, though, he was right about one thing—this practice had an aura of failure about it.

He had said these were appointment hours—what suc-

cessful doctor needed to have hours on a Saturday afternoon? But in the time she'd been here there hadn't even
been the whiff of a patient, and there was no receptionist
at the desk and no practice nurse in evidence. Evidently
those roles were covered by that neat but pathetic little sign,
PLEASE RING AND SIT DOWN.

Yes, she definitely felt sorry for him!

He was scowling at her now and looking at his watch.
Clearly he wanted her to go. Fifteen years ago she'd have
done it, too, turning tail and running like a rabbit, but she
was much stronger now. More stubborn, too. There was far
more to her than the 'pretty blonde princess' he had jeered
at. There always *had* been more underneath or she'd never
have made it through medical school, internship and residency, including a year in obstetrics before she had found
greater satisfaction in family practice.

'No coffee,' she said, crisply, still refusing to admit defeat. 'OK. But fill me in a bit, Luke, please. Last time I
saw you, you'd...' Again, how to put this tactfully? Perhaps
you couldn't. 'Dropped out of school and were working as
a motorcycle mechanic for a living. Then you left town,
didn't you? Now you're a specialist in family practice. It
can't have been an easy road.'

'You got that right.' He gave a short, wry laugh, and it
wasn't one of amusement. 'I had to finish high school, college, medical school—although hard study was the least of
it, in fact. And there was a detour when I tried endocrinology for a year and a half, then decided—well, that I
wanted more variety. But when something happens to turn
your life around that tends to be a pretty strong motivating
force for whatever you have to get through next.'

'What happened to you, Luke?' she asked. 'I—I don't
think I ever heard.' She tried vainly to sift through impres-
sions and tales that were years out of date. 'Was it a...a
religious conversion, or—'

He laughed impatiently. 'A religious conversion?'

'People do have them.'

'Why that, though? Why was that your first guess? Oh, my clothes?' He hazarded—and correctly, she realised, analysing her own thought track. 'You thought I'd still be in black leather?'

'No, of course not. I—'

'In that case, why are *you* dressed in that very nicely cut navy linen suit? Why aren't you still wearing those little teenage sundresses that *just* about let the light through to—'

He stopped abruptly and laughed again. 'Never mind! I dress like this in the stubborn hope that it'll do something useful for my image in this town. So far it hasn't. But fortunately I feel fairly comfortable this way these days. Back to your initial question, though. Not a religious conversion. Let's see. What was the real turning point? When I was…uh…persuaded that leaving town was a good idea? No, difficult as that was, it was after that in New Jersey. My kid died,' he finished harshly.

'Oh, Luke!' she gasped.

'It's all right. It would have been worse if he'd lived. He was premature and his mother was a junkie. We had a bike accident and it brought on labour seventeen weeks early, before any hope of survival. And now, if you don't mind, I'll say a very courteous and very professional goodbye. Unless I'm very much mistaken, I'm about to have a patient. Don't worry, though, I doubt she's one your father would mind your losing to this practice. She's highly unlikely to pay.'

'*What*?' she gasped, appalled at both his rude, outrageous insinuations and at his callous dismissal of his dead child. 'As if that matters to me! I'm perfectly happy to work with Medicaid patients or accept payment in instalments.'

She was gearing up to rage at him further, but how could she? He was completely ignoring her now, and had gone to the door to open it. A badly dressed, very pregnant and almost completely toothless woman of about forty or so was waddling uncomfortably along the cracked cement path that ran down the side of the house, evidently having emerged from the large, rusty and very battered-looking car now parked at the kerb.

It must have been the squeak and slam of the car door which had alerted Luke to her arrival.

'Hi, Karen,' he said to her cheerfully with a smile. Francesca remembered that smile. It hadn't changed in fifteen years and neither, evidently, had she, because it still made her stomach flip and her pulses leap, even when it wasn't turned in her direction. And even when she was swimming in a soup of appalled fury at the man. 'Come on in.'

'Oh, Dr Luke.' The woman beamed in relief, her coarse face softening wonderfully. 'It's good of you to see me. I'm really not feeling that great today.'

And this was an understatement because ten seconds later she had fallen to the floor in the full throes of an eclamptic seizure.

Luke and Francesca both recognised it for what it was at once, but he was the one who took charge. 'Hold her. I'll get a bite plate. Don't let her do any damage to herself. Her blood pressure is probably over the moon. I've got Valium.'

He was pulling keys from his pocket and had disappeared down the corridor to open the door of his small dispensary.

'Ambulance?' Francesca said quickly.

'Yes, because we may have to deliver her.' He passed her the bite plate and she inserted it with some difficulty. The woman was still in seizure.

'How close to term is she?'

'A week, two at the most. Can't remember exactly.'

He downed a full bottle of orange juice in a casual sort of way, then bolted what looked like a peanut butter sandwich as if his life depended on it.

Eating seemed inappropriate under the circumstances,

and she said with a note of accusation, 'But, surely…
Haven't you been seeing her for prenatal care?'

'When she manages to keep an appointment. She hasn't
for about four weeks. I think her boyfriend must have been
out of town with the car. Don't let's waste time on her
history. Call the ambulance!' Both sandwich and juice had
already disappeared.

'Phone?'

'Right there.'

He pointed to the desk, then vanished into another room
to wash his hands. She dialled 911, fumbling a little over
the details. What was the street address of this place? 'State
Street,' she gabbled. 'The shabby white house. The Wilde
place.'

'Number 135,' he supplied for her tersely, back again,
bringing the Valium and administering it through the intravenous line he had deftly put in while she gave the rest of
the details that the emergency service required.

Within five minutes the seizures had stopped and they
could safely remove the bite plate that had prevented her
from swallowing or cutting her tongue, but Luke had had
to give her a large dose of the drug.

'She's pretty out of it. We'll need to monitor her very
carefully.'

'And the baby.'

'And the baby,' he agreed.

'We need to move her, too,' Francesca said now.

'It's not going to be easy,' he pointed out. 'At her last
visit, she tipped the scales at…can't remember. Must have
been 240 pounds. I hope you're stronger than you look.'

Hell, did he have to make everything sound like an accusation?

Fortunately, *he* was strong. They rolled Karen onto a
blanket, then slid her into the surgery and managed to lift
her to the table, with a moment of swaying assistance from
the woman herself. This gave much easier access to the

blood-pressure cuff and other equipment, and meant that an internal examination would be easier, too.

'Is she in labour?' Francesca asked.

'Hard to tell. She's coming round a bit now. Let's ask. Karen?' Only Francesca realised now that he wasn't quite saying Karen, but Karon. No, Caron. Sharon Baron's sister, if Preston Stock had got his relationships right. 'Caron, you're OK now.' He was shaking her gently. 'The ambulance is on its way. Are you having any pains?'

Groggily, she frowned. 'Was.'

'OK, well, we're going to listen to the baby now, check your blood pressure and feel your cervix to see if you've started to dilate.'

Francesca took the blood-pressure cuff and inflated it, while Luke prepared to do the internal. One-eighty over one-oh-five. As he had said, that was over the moon. Her face and limbs were swollen, too, because of fluid retention, and it was likely that the placenta wasn't functioning as it should. Luke had finished his exam. 'Sixty per cent effaced. No dilatation. You're not going to have a baby just yet, then, Caron.'

'No?' she managed. 'Do I…go home?'

'Oh, no, my dear, you don't do that!'

He was listening to the baby's heartbeat now with a special stethoscope. For all this place's shabbiness, he did seem to have the equipment at least.

'Heart rate's OK,' he commented. 'Hang on, though…' Caron was grimacing now, and then a groan broke from her puffy lips. 'Pain, Caron?'

She nodded, then bellowed groggily. It subsided within a minute and she lapsed into a drug-induced doze again.

'Looks like labour has started,' Luke said. 'That's probably good.'

'As long as it doesn't stress the baby.'

'We'll worry about that if it happens. Meanwhile, I'm putting more fluid in this IV.'

He did it quickly and efficiently while Francesca kept listening to the baby's heartbeat, checked Caron's blood pressure again and ran through her other vital signs. Her breathing wasn't great, but it would do.

'OK, fluid's going in,' Luke said, then he taped the IV line more firmly in place.

Once again Francesca noticed that his equipment was in good condition and easily to hand. It earned her very grudging respect. With everything else so shabby, she'd half expected to find makeshift tape and no saline.

And with his level of hostility, she was almost starting to *want* to believe the worst of him!

But this was a level of pettiness that neither of them could afford right now.

To an observer it might seem wrong to be putting in fluid when Caron Baron was already so swollen, but this fluid should go to where it was most needed—the starved placenta.

'Looks like another contraction,' Luke said a few minutes later. 'That's…what, only about five minutes?'

'About. Wasn't counting.'

'No. OK, steady, Caron, we're just listening to the baby again.' He looked a question at Francesca. How was the heart rate?

'Slowing,' she answered, hating to have to say it. 'Perceptibly. Coming back up now that the contraction is ebbing.'

'We need to get her right hip up. Her position's not great.'

With difficulty they managed to slide folded towels under Caron's vast hip, but five minutes later another contraction came and the baby's heart rate dipped even further.

For the first time Francesca was really worried. 'How long does the ambulance take these days from Wayans Falls?'

'Still half an hour. They haven't done much to improve the road. It still winds.'

'And I called, what, fifteen minutes ago? What if there's a delay in their response? If—if that heart rate stops coming back up can we section her?'

He closed his eyes and she was startled at the sight of those two crescents of thick dark lashes. She remembered them!

'It'd be gruesome,' he said.

'But *could* we?'

'I have muscle relaxant, I have nitrous oxide. It wouldn't be enough to completely mask the pain of the incision, but the Valium would help. We could use a little narcotic if we had to, although to depress the baby with something like that…'

'If we can avoid it we should,' Francesca agreed.

'And I haven't done a section for six months.'

'But I have, and I did a year of obstetrics,' she said. 'That part I could handle.'

'She's obese.'

'Yes, it wouldn't be fast.'

'It'd have to be.'

'Low transverse incision?'

'Midline,' he corrected. 'Her fibroids are pretty bad.'

'Oh, great! Great…and you say she won't be completely under.'

'I'll give you as much as I can but, as I said, narcotics are iffy, and if the baby is already fading…'

'The baby… My baby…' Caron moaned suddenly, her eyes swimming open.

Luke pulled Francesca aside, one hand massaging Caron's shoulder fiercely although she could tell he wasn't even aware of it, and said to her in low, urgent tones, 'She wants it, Chess, she wants it badly. I know that's hard to believe… It's her first. She's forty-one, she's dirt-poor, she lives in a broken-down mobile home and her boyfriend's half-cracked, but she wants it so much. She's actually been reading books on child-care—and her reading's about fourth-grade level. She's been asking my advice about feeding and potty-training. We can't let her lose it.'

'I—I know. But the ambulance will be here, Luke. We don't need to worry. I don't know why we're even talking about it like this.'

'Because this is real medicine. Look, another contraction's coming already.'

This time he took the stethoscope and listened intently. With the woman's vast girth, it was hard to pinpoint the beat. 'Low,' he said. 'Thirties. Forties.'

'Too low. Is it coming back up?'

He listened again. The contraction was ending, with Caron twisting on the table and giving a last moan. 'Eighties,' he said. 'A baseline rate in the eighties now.'

They looked at each other, both knowing it was way too low. A good foetal heart rate should be about double that of an adult. A rate per minute above a hundred was the minimum desirable level, and to have it in the 140s or even higher was what they wanted.

'The ambulance will be here,' Francesca insisted shrilly. 'Five minutes now. Maybe less. We couldn't get her set up for a Caesarean in that time, anyway. We'd need… I mean, is there anyone else in this town? A nurse?'

'A couple. Ginny Traynor works down at Wayans Falls Hospital. Betsy Schwab's done OR nursing, but she hasn't worked in several years. I'll call Ginny.' He threw the dispensary keys to her. 'You get out the drugs and the rest of the gear.'

He picked up the phone, but as she went along to the dispensary and store-room she didn't hear him talking. When she got back he reported, 'No one's home. Weather's too nice.' Just then Caron moaned again. 'Another one?' he muttered. 'Hell, they're getting to be only three or four minutes apart now!'

And this time the baseline heart rate rebounded only as high as the sixties, while during the contraction itself it was even lower than it had been before.

'We've got to do it, haven't we?' Francesca said, her voice high. 'We can't keep waiting.'

They looked at each other with the same mute understanding that had been in their faces fifteen years ago—that night he'd kissed her. In a sudden flood of realisation, she thought incredulously, he really wanted that kiss. Almost as much as I did. It wasn't just a cheap thrill for him. He must have...really wanted me then. No, surely not!

The flash of insight faded and she doubted it at once—as she doubted her ability to undertake this major operation now, in a rural practice surgery, with the wrong anaesthesia, inadequate help, and an obese first-time mother who was forty-one years old, with fibroids.

Then they both heard the wail of the ambulance siren.

'Oh, thank God!' Francesca breathed. The keening sound was incredibly sweet to her ears.

But Luke shook his head tightly. 'She can't wait another half an hour. We're going to have to do it here and then move her straight down.'

He didn't wait for her reply, but was lunging out into the waiting room and through the side door to hail the ambulance and direct its bumpy journey across the lawn. Two uniformed ambulance officers jumped out and brought a stretcher.

'The patient's inside,' Luke said, 'but you can't take her yet. We're going to have to section her here.'

Caron moaned. She was having another contraction. Francesca was listening, her stomach churning. 'The heart rate's not going back up,' she said. 'It's...it's sluggish. Erratic.'

'OK,' Luke said. 'Let's get her undressed, draped and tubed *now*. You'll do it, Francesca, while I handle the anaesthesia and whatever else I can manage. You guys...' he turned to the ambulance officers '…scrub and assist. We're winging it here.'

Francesca felt sick.

She had done C-sections before, dozens of them, but always under controlled conditions and always with the right staff, the right equipment and the knowledge that there was someone more experienced than she was close at hand. She'd never done one on a patient this obese, and this time *she* was the expert. Luke hadn't done this operation in six months.

Somehow, though, he was the steady one—the one who took ultimate control. The ambulance officers were as nervous as Francesca was. Luke had been working on removing Caron Baron's clothes, cutting unceremoniously with surgical scissors when he couldn't lift or pull, but now he handed that task over to Ray McCallum and Barry Linz.

A minute later he had the nitrous oxide ready to go in, and then intubated Caron, extending her head and flexing her neck forward. He managed the task with deft efficiency, then checked that her breath sounds were bilateral and equal, checked over her belly to rule out the slight possibility that the tube had gone into her stomach, taped the tube in place and measured it—twenty centimetres at the lips.

Meanwhile, Francesca had been swabbing the patient's now-bared abdomen with antiseptic and frantically trying to visualise the whole procedure in her mind. What was going to be difficult about doing it here? What was going to be different?

'Retractors?' she said.

'A couple,' Luke answered. 'Probably not as big as you'd like for this job.' He added seconds later, 'OK, she's as out as she's going to get, Francesca, and everything's draped. Let's get to work.'

At first Francesca was very aware of the different circumstances of this surgery—fewer people than usual, no

seasoned OR nurses, not quite the right equipment for some
tasks. As she got fully into the work, though, she forgot
about the fact that this was not how a Caesarean delivery
was normally performed, and focused only on what was in
front of her.

Skin, fat—which took time to cut through—blood, muscle, the stretched uterine wall. Luke was right. The retractors weren't quite big enough, but Ray McCallum skilfully
put them in place under her guidance, keeping everything
as far as he could from where she needed to work.

'OK,' she said at last. 'We'll have a baby in a minute.'
Then she had pulled him out—a small boy, very blue and
limp and not yet breathing spontaneously.

Luke suctioned the nose and mouth at once, and again,
but there was still no effort to breathe, and just the slightest
of movements in the small limbs.

'Bag him?' Barry Linz suggested, but Luke shook his
head and suctioned again.

'The heart rate's good now. He should do fine...' But
the seconds were ticking by and nothing happened. Luke
shook his head. 'No, you can't quite get it, can you, little
guy? OK, yes, bag him.' Suddenly, after Barry had worked
over the blue, screwed-up little face with the ambu-bag for
some seconds, there was a jerky, staccato cry that soon
strengthened into a more lusty bawl, and the baby's torso
and, slowly, his extremities began to turn from blue to pink.

'Oh, thank God!' Francesca breathed.

He was a mess, of course, covered in blood and ver-
nix—the cheesy white coating that babies had in the
womb—but he looked so much stronger now.

'Five or six pounds,' Luke guessed. He was placing the
baby in the warmed transport isolette from the ambulance
to preserve body heat and allow more detailed assessment
of his condition. Heart rate, reflexes, colour and breathing.
His Apgar score was five at two minutes since birth, which
indicated what the dipping heart rate *in utero* had sug-

gested—that the uterine environment had not been the best by the end. At six minutes, though, when Luke assessed it again, the score was nine, which gave a rough yet promising prognosis for his future.

Francesca delivered the placenta, studying it carefully. Intact. Healthy. Not huge. The baby had stopped crying already. 'Groggy,' Luke said, putting silver nitrate drops in the little boy's eyes. 'From the anaesthesia. And the Valium. But alive and basically healthy.'

For the first time in fifteen minutes Francesca became aware of her surroundings once more. She realised how stiff she was in almost every muscle, her fingers were trembling and her whole hand ached. And there was still a good half-hour, closer to forty-five minutes, of stitching to do because she'd worked quickly on the incision and needed to check carefully now for bleeding vessels.

Now, though, it was safe to give Caron a dose of narcotics, which should remove any lingering awareness of pain. Then, as soon as the incision was fully closed, they'd need to transport her and the baby directly to Wayans Falls, monitoring both of them closely during the journey.

An hour and a half later it was all over. Baby Baron was having his first bath in the hospital nursery, while still being carefully monitored in case his mother's acute illness and the drugs she had been given posed any further risk. Caron Baron was being wheeled to the ICU and would also need close monitoring.

While eclampsia was the obvious cause of her seizure, and her grogginess could be explained by this seizure and by the medication given to control it, nobody wanted to take chances. There were other possibilities and they needed to be ruled out. She had been started on magnesium sulphate, too, as her eclampsia could pose a threat for up to seventy-two hours after delivery.

Francesca and Luke emerged from the Wayans Falls hospital's emergency room together, and only now had a

chance to peel off the disposable caps, masks and gowns
they'd put on for the surgery. There was a clock on the
wall just above the large waste-bin, and it read four forty-
five. The whole afternoon had gone.

Rather fuzzily, Francesca suggested, 'Shall we get a taxi
back? Or is there a bus?'

He shook his head. 'Last bus left at four.'

He reached a hand up and loosened his tie, then pulled
it off altogether and undid the top button of his shirt to
expose a neck which, even this early in the season, was a
healthy outdoor brown. He'd always had easy-tanning skin,
Francesca remembered, in contrast to her own fair and well-
protected complexion. She noticed, too, that his collarbone
and temples were misted with sweat, and was a little surprised.

There had been no time for any awareness of him as
they'd worked over his patient, but now it returned in full
force—that weird sense, like a double-exposed photograph,
that she was seeing the old Luke, the hot-blooded eighteen-
year-old layered beneath this new far more seasoned and
outwardly safer man.

'A taxi, then, I guess.' She had to struggle to remember
the subject at hand. 'It'll be cheaper if we share.'

But he shook his head. 'I'm not coming. Not yet. I need
to eat. Also, I want to stay until Caron's awake and not so
out of it, and that might take a couple of hours. She'll have
questions and concerns.'

'Right. OK.' She nodded, then added impulsively,
'That's nice of you, Luke. A lot of doctors aren't that caring
these days. I—I enjoyed working with you, by the way,
and I thought we made a very efficient team.'

There was a beat of ugly silence, then he said heavily,
'Did you, now? And you think I'm *caring*, do you? Well,
grateful though I am for your patronising approval, let me
tell you straight out—that's the first and last time we'll ever
practise medicine together so if you have any rosy little

ideas to the contrary you can get them out of your head right now.'

She felt as if he'd slapped her in the face, his cold, deliberate rudeness a horrible affront. His reception of her two hours ago at his surgery had been rude and angry, too, but somehow she had thought—and had felt herself—that their successful delivery of Caron's baby together had cut through that and brought something more important to the fore—a professional kinship which she knew she would need in a small town.

His repudiation of any such bond was so shocking that she couldn't even react, and simply stared at him in stunned silence, leaving the field wide open for him to have the last word.

Which he did.

'I'll see you around, I'm sure, Francesca.' The drawled tone made it quite clear that he felt no pleasure at the prospect and, as if to underline this, he added after a tiny pause, 'But I'll try to make it as infrequently as possible.'

Turning on his heel, he strode back into the emergency room, and all Francesca could do was numbly watch him.

CHAPTER THREE

FIVE minutes into her quite expensive and very solitary taxi ride from Wayans Falls back to Darrensberg the numbness wore off and Francesca was seething.

Luke Wilde had more than a chip on his shoulder, he had a positive rock slide. His father's practice had failed for some reason, and now his was failing too—perhaps every bit of Preston's gossip was true—and he was taking it out on her purely because *her* father had been a success.

For most of the journey she plotted not merely a continuation of the old family rivalry but an augmentation of it. By fair means or foul, she vowed, she would drive Luke out of business, have him selling that shabby mansion of his and slinking out of town. Or, better yet, crawling to her and begging her for a junior partnership in *her* magnificent practice...which she would refuse to even consider until he had begged much, much harder, at which point she just might graciously concede.

Might. Maybe, even then, she wouldn't. Maybe she'd buy the shabby mansion herself and run *two* practices here, with whole fleets of doctors under her command like navvies on a ship, while Luke would be licking his wounds in some three-walled shack, wishing he could even dream of being one of them.

It was at this point that the poison of her anger began to leach from her system. Unfortunately, most unfortunately, she just wasn't that kind of person. She was far too well brought up to ever stoop to such levels. In fact, she was really quite saintly, to the point where, as soon as he'd apologised adequately—no, OK, apologised *effusively*—she would generously forgive and forget the whole thing. Help him get on his feet a bit, perhaps.

Hang on, though, that wasn't right either because—as a genuine emotional equilibrium began to return—there was still one key fact that didn't ring true here. Luke's practice was failing, and it *shouldn't* be, should it?

She had seen herself what a good doctor he seemed to be. Efficient, knowledgeable, unflappable, concerned—and with that extra indefinable *talent* for medicine that she'd encountered before and instinctively recognised, though she couldn't ever put a finger on quite what it consisted of. She didn't even know if she had it herself. She was convinced that Luke did, though.

And yet—as the taxi drove up State Street and deposited her outside her elegant house—Darrensberg didn't trust him, and didn't want him.

She paid the taxi driver and let herself inside, thinking of what Preston Stock had said over lunch. 'People don't forget.' Was it that simple? Darrensberg wouldn't forgive the son for the father's scandalous failure? Or did the problem go back further and run deeper than that?

For the first time she wished she'd questioned her father more closely when he'd spoken of the Wilde practice over the past few years, wished she'd attempted to mine beneath his often emotion-coloured phrasing, gone down to Florida for a snatched weekend now that he'd convalesced—to talk in a serious, practical way about Darrensberg and her future here.

She had been so naïve fifteen years ago. Which of all those long-ago rumours had been true? Which had even *existed*? That rich, adolescent imagination of hers might have created half of them itself out of a few cryptic words.

Wilde by name and wild by nature. Had he been? He had mentioned a baby today that had died, born of a drug-addicted mother, and he had said it all so callously and casually that she almost hadn't taken in the context of the words at the time.

He had been answering her question about what had turned his life around, and it had been that—a very traumatic event. His prematurely born child dying after an accident. He *must* have cared then. His callousness today must have been all on the surface, but evidently that was the level on which the town had judged him.

Darrensberg didn't think that he had really changed. Was that it? She desperately wanted to at least know the truth for herself, and it suddenly occurred to her that perhaps Darrensberg was right. Perhaps the town had good reason to mistrust him. Did he have a drug habit?

Those disturbing moments of chemistry today hinted that she wasn't as objective on the issue as she should be, and this angered her.

Crazy! I won't be blinded by such a thing, as I was at fifteen. For heaven's sake, I'm a mature professional now. If Luke *is* doing something wrong then, yes, he'll have to take the consequences!

She combed through every bit of his behaviour in her mind but nothing stood out, unless it was that odd, inappropriate downing of lunch right in those critical moments after Caron's collapse. That was addictive behaviour, wasn't it? A refusal to postpone the gratification of one's bodily needs?

But, surely, his skill during the afternoon's emergency, another part of her clamoured.

'I'm getting nowhere with this,' she muttered aloud to the hallway, crowded with boxes and furniture. 'I don't know why I even care!'

Waking up in her old turret room the next morning to the aura of sunshine and the sound of spring birds was wonderful. The room hadn't changed in fifteen years. It was still a shrine to her innocent teenage years, and for a few weeks more she planned to keep it that way. Then, though, there would be changes. You had to grow up. She was thirty now, and her tastes had changed a lot.

She planned to move into her parents' master suite, once she'd revamped it, and make this turret room a study, while Chris's room would remain a spare room and her sister, Louise's…well, she wasn't sure. Her mother had used it for sewing.

The whole place was really far too big for her. She did hope to marry at some stage, and then there would be children. So far it hadn't happened, and she wasn't quite sure why. During her years of study and training she'd been through a series of rather tepid, intellectual relationships, which had done a lot for her confidence in her intelligence but not much else, and she'd abandoned the last of these relationships two months ago.

Rob Hayes had agreed with her that it wasn't going anywhere. She was heading north to a practice of her own, and he was about to join a group practice outside Washington, DC. Neither of them had found the prospect of the geographical distance a sudden and compelling reason to seek greater commitment. So here she was alone, with strong professional ambitions and nagging unanswered questions about her personal life.

What was she looking for that she hadn't found yet?

Nagging or not, she decided, they didn't warrant dwelling on today. There was far too much to do…. Like the rest of her unpacking, and shopping for supplies. She hadn't even bought milk or bread last night, and Preston appeared to have cleared out the fridge with commendable thoroughness. For dinner she had just sent out for pizza.

Now she was hungry for breakfast, with juice and cereal and coffee. Cold leftover pizza didn't appeal.

Accordingly, she showered and dressed and let herself out the back door to go to the car which was parked in the garage, backing onto a rear alley that was actually more like a country lane. She had slept in, so it was after nine, and the town's day was already well started. Some people were going to church. People who hadn't mowed their lawns yesterday were mowing them today. From not too far off came the sound of energetic hammering and the shriek of nails coming loose as wooden boards were pulled up. It all echoed rather musically in the clear spring mountain air.

Not too far off was Luke's place, she worked out, and curiosity got the better of her almost immediately. That need to find out the truth about him still nagged at her. She was a stubbornly tidy person and didn't like loose ends.

She set off up the back lane. It was a sunny morning, and therefore faintly plausible that she was simply going for a walk. In any case, with all that hammering going on, he was unlikely to notice her.

He did, though, almost at once. He had stopped for a rest, surrounded by the litter of old wood from the sagging porch he was tearing up. She watched him as he surveyed what he'd done, then wiped his forearm across his brow and put the hammer down.

There was a faucet attached to the rear garage and he came over, cheap plastic cup in hand, to pour himself a drink, and that was when he caught sight of her as she quickly began to walk again. Not quickly enough, unfortunately.

'Hi,' he said, with a very sour intonation.

'You're… You've made a good start,' she said with determined brightness. Any hostility in this relationship was *not* going to come from her. Not yet, anyway.

'It'll go faster when I have help.' Not quite so terse, this.

'Faster? You're nearly finished.'

'Tearing it up, yes. I'm hoping to get a new floor down today.'

'You've got carpenters coming.' She was simply making conversation.

This morning he looked disturbingly like the eighteen-year-old she remembered so vividly, wearing a pale blue T-shirt and tight, faded jeans instead of yesterday's carefully professional attire. Leather or jeans, that was all she had ever seen him in back then—all he'd ever worn in her fantasies, too. But that was fifteen or sixteen years ago. The reality shouldn't be so overwhelming.

'Carpenters?' he was saying. 'You could call them that. They're just local men helping me with the work to pay off their medical bills, and unfortunately I expect they'll all do that before the job's quite done. My patients tomorrow, if I have any, may have to negotiate a few holes.'

'Are you this bitter all the time?' she blurted. 'I have to say it doesn't suit you, Luke. You didn't used to be bitter.'

He shrugged. 'Perhaps you just bring out the worst in me, honey.' It was a cruel drawl.

'Me? Why *me*?' she demanded wildly. 'Till yesterday, you hadn't seen me for fifteen years!'

Already—again—a simple exchange had escalated. She had been enquiring in a well-meaning way about what he was doing, and now he was *attacking* her!

'OK,' she went on in a fury, not caring what she said, 'so I probably drove you crazy back then mooning over you, but—'

'*Mooning* over me?' he growled. 'You never mooned over me, did you, Chess?' He was looking oddly alert suddenly, and his eyes had narrowed with wary curiosity.

She wasn't embarrassed. She wasn't going to play it down. It had been, after all, fifteen years ago. Those powerful, turbulent emotions were as distant now as if they'd belonged to someone else, and confessing to them impulsively in the course of an angry exchange was by far the best way of removing any lingering vestige of their power.

'Oh, God, of course I did!' she told him crossly. 'I'm surprised it wasn't crushingly obvious to you. I was nuts about you. If I so much as glimpsed you it made my day.'

'Yeah? You never spoke to me unless I asked you a direct question, and then you squeaked out the minimum you could get away with,' he challenged, and there was an untamable light in his blue eyes that she remembered very well. 'You never looked at me. You shrank back if I came too close. You always acted as if you were terrified of me.'

'Yes! Yes, I did! All that! Because I thought you were so wonderful that it just froze me up. Don't you know *anything* about well-sheltered teenage girls, Luke?'

'Evidently not! So you fancied me for a while there— until your nice upbringing brought you to your senses.' He gave an odd laugh. 'Well, I'll be—'

'Don't make too much of it,' she told him crisply, not deigning to address that cheap jibe about her upbringing. 'It's half a lifetime ago now. I was another person then.'

'True. As I was.' He was still watching her with those electric eyes. Angry eyes? She couldn't tell. Wary, for sure. 'So I expect you've forgotten the time I kissed you?' he drawled.

'Forgotten? Ha!' She laughed impatiently. 'Not the sort of thing girls forget, Luke, their first kiss.'

'Was it? Yours?'

'Of course! Why? Did you think I—?'

'No need to get indignant,' he drawled. 'You were…quite good at it, that's all.'

Their eyes met and she flushed, embarrassed as she hadn't been until now. 'I doubt that,' she protested crisply.

'Believe me, Chess, you were. And, as it *wasn't* my first kiss or my last, I'm in a position to know.'

'Well, thank you,' she drawled in turn, then added, even more cynically, 'I guess.'

'Sure. Take it as a compliment.' He scowled suddenly, and it was like the sun disappearing behind a cloud. 'It's probably the only one you'll get from me.'

'So we're back to that, are we?' she said angrily. 'I really don't have to take it, you know!'

'No. Fine. Don't,' he agreed shortly.

'God, you *are* bitter!'

'Sure,' he agreed again. 'Very. I find it a useful emotion. Motivating. Strengthening.'

'Maybe in the short term,' she countered with sharp conviction, 'but I'd think before taking it regularly as a tonic, if I were you, Luke. It's like some drugs. If it builds up in your system it's a poison, and it can kill you.'

'Perhaps,' he answered darkly, 'but I've reached the conclusion that there are worse ways to die.'

The last word again. What could she say to top *that* little piece of brutal, aggressive cynicism? Nothing! She simply shook her head helplessly, turned and went back the way she had come, not even bothering to maintain the pretence of going for a walk.

He didn't say anything more either, and behind her, after a minute, she heard the sound of hammering again. It seemed louder, and when he pulled the loosened, splintered boards away the nails shrieked like creatures from a nightmare.

I won't come this way again! she vowed as she climbed into her car, switched on the engine and shot it aggressively into reverse. Clearly, if there's anything to be found out about Luke I'm *not* going to get it from him! Unfortunately, it wouldn't be very professional to seek out the gossip, but I guess I'm bound to hear the truth eventually. Meanwhile, I needn't see him or think about him or his pitiful little practice at all, if I don't want to.

Except that two minutes later she discovered she was wrong about this. Driving down the street into town, she found they'd changed the roads a little. She'd vaguely noticed it yesterday on the way in but it hadn't affected her in that direction. This way, it did.

There was a new one-way section along one side of the triangle where State Street, Route 19 and Main Street ran untidily into each other, evidently to cope with peak-season traffic flow, but it meant an awkward detour to bring her south on Route 19, where the big supermarket was. She immediately realised how much easier it would be to avoid the one-way bit by going up State Street and turning right on Hudson, but going up State Street meant, of course, going past Luke's.

I won't do it! was her first thought. I just won't!

But then she'd be letting him affect her—*inconvenience* her, actually—on a very regular basis, and that idea was unthinkable, especially now that she'd despatched the ghost of her long ago crush once and for all. So she had no choice. She'd be driving past his house almost daily. The knowledge didn't do much for her morning, and she shopped in a very bad mood.

'Here's your coffee, honey,' Betty Mayberry said brightly to Francesca, bustling into her office the next morning at nine.

She hadn't knocked. Francesca found this faintly irritating but didn't want to say so for risk of giving offence. Mrs Mayberry had been her father's receptionist for twenty-five years, as loyal as an old family retainer in a period English novel.

Also, as it happened, Francesca didn't want coffee. She'd had a cup half an hour ago over breakfast, and that would be quite enough until about four, at which time a second one might be nice to lift her energy for a last hour of appointments.

She said as much, in a polite and pleasant way. Mrs Mayberry nodded and smiled. 'Your father always had coffee at nine. He said it got him into the day.'

'I remember.' Francesca chuckled. 'He was like a bear with a sore head if he didn't get his coffee.'

'Oh, he was, wasn't he?' Mrs Mayberry agreed, depositing the coffee on Francesca's desk as if she'd already forgotten the beginning of the conversation. Then she stepped back. 'Goodness, the picture you make, sitting there! I can't countenance that you're a doctor now!'

'Well, I am,' Francesca replied briskly, 'and I hope Dad's patients can "countenance" it, or I'll lose them all to Dr Wilde!'

She meant it as a joke, but Mrs Mayberry was frowning now, her eyes anxious and her lips pursed.

'Oh, don't worry about him, dear! He won't be around much longer.'

'Oh, he won't?'

'Yes… It's sad, really. I almost feel sorry for him… After the way his father's practice failed, too, a couple of years ago… But, after all, he's brought it all on himself.'

'Brought it—? What do you mean, Mrs Mayberry?'

'Drugs!' she hissed. 'Didn't Dr Stock tell you?'

'Well, yes, he mentioned a rumour, but I—'

'I've thought of reporting him, but for Margaret Wilde's sake… It's not going to be necessary, anyway. He has scarcely any patients, and the types he does have—well, they probably all use drugs themselves! Anyway, it's tragic, really. Like father, like son, I always say. I know you never heard about it all, honey,' she finished now, firm and kind, 'but, as you say, you're a doctor now. He killed a woman, you know.'

'*Luke*?'

'No, not Luke. His father, of course. She bled to death up in the woods in some awful mobile home, having her baby. And I ask you—what was he doing, delivering her up there in insanitary conditions when there's a perfectly good hospital half an hour away?'

'So that's what it was? I—I had no idea.' Luke with a drug problem, and now this story.

'Well, your parents would have made sure of that. You were such an innocent.'

'Still, though…' She was groping, shocked. Disasters did happen. Doctors lost patients. Why was Mrs Mayberry so sure it was James Wilde's fault? 'If she'd left it too late to get to the hospital... Post-partum haemorrhage can't be predicted.'

'Oh, but there was far more to it than that! Luke Wilde was the baby's father, they say. He was there when it all happened. Drunk. And on drugs even then, too.'

'And d-did the baby die as well?' Francesca heard herself saying, as if her voice were coming from far away, remembering too clearly Luke's own words on Saturday.

'Oh, heavens, yes! It was far too early. Oh, yes! The baby died.'

A sound came from outside and Mrs Mayberry's face brightened. 'Do you hear the door, honey? That'll be your very first patient. Barbara Wiggs. Now, you'll like Barbara, she's delightful. You won't have met her. She's had a lot of trouble with—'

'Thanks, Mrs Mayberry,' Francesca interrupted, more firmly than she felt inside. 'I've already looked at Mrs Wiggs's chart. But just tell Dixie to give me five more minutes, will you, before she sends her into the examining room?'

'Well, of course.' Mrs Mayberry beamed. 'You'll need time to drink that coffee.'

Francesca did drink it, too, feeling numb and desperate at the same time and grateful for the steadying effect of the bitter, biting-hot brew. What Mrs Mayberry had said—it couldn't be true! It was so horrible, so sordid! The complicity between father and son, the flagrant medical malpractice of delivering a baby in the wrong conditions simply in order to hush up the birth, the suggestion that drugs and alcohol were somehow involved...

Mrs Mayberry's way of telling it, too, had been a shock—the matter-of-fact disapproval, the lack of any sympathy for the labouring woman herself or for the baby, the smug conviction that Luke's newly resurrected practice would soon fail completely, and in the meantime any patients he saw and misdiagnosed didn't count because they were only 'that type'.

Francesca had always seen her father's loyal secretary as such a sweet, harmless person, and had agreed without a minute's thought to Mom's suggestion that dear Betty stay on for a six-month transition period before her retirement. Dad would have fretted about any other plan.

And, of course, there's no need to question that decision just because she's relaying a scandal that particularly upsets me, Francesca realised now, a little more calmly.

Why *did* the scandal upset her so much, though? *Because she believed it?*

Did she? She didn't *want* to…but Luke himself had spoken of a dead baby and a drug-addicted mother. He hadn't mentioned his own drug use, though. As if he would, to another doctor! But why do I so badly want to believe in him?

She didn't have time to answer this question now. There was a light tap at the door, and practice nurse Dixie Andrews put her artfully untidy red-gold head around the door to say, 'I've shown Mrs Wiggs into the pink room, Dr Brady.'

'Thanks, Dixie.'

She stood up at once and picked up the chart. This was her first morning in a practice she might run for the rest of her career, and she didn't want to set a precedent by running late at this stage.

Two hours later she began to realise that running late was unavoidable, and it wasn't her fault either. People had evidently been saving up their complaints—or else the practice was far too successful for its own good. She'd already had a full schedule at the outset, and now eight people had called, asking to be squeezed in. Mrs Mayberry said that Dad *always* fitted everyone in.

Additionally, people wanted to chat. They wondered how 'old Dr Brady' was doing, and it was odd at first to hear him referred to this way and to realise that *she* was 'Dr Brady' now. A few of them remembered her from years ago and wanted to tell her at length how adult and clever and competent she looked now.

Some of them were newer residents, *didn't* remember her and were curious about the fact that Frank Brady's daughter from New York had taken over. At times she had to be quite firm in cutting short the flow, although it was nice to hear all these good wishes. She would have rather liked to tape some of the conversation and send it to Preston Stock, who had been so wittily scathing about Darrensberg having forgotten her.

Then, of course, after all this chat there was the nuisance—to some of her patients it was clearly a nuisance—of actually having to deal with whatever medical problem had brought them to the doctor in the first place.

She diagnosed three ear infections in young children and two cases of Influenza B in adults. She removed a leaf fragment from a teenager's eye. She diagnosed pregnancy in a young woman who thought she 'must have that chronic fatigue syndrome' and was very happy to discover that she didn't. That was a nice moment!

She conducted initial examinations on several patients, which then led to the suggestion of an endometrial biopsy for the analysis of tissue in the uterus of a twenty-seven-year-old waitress, some cryotherapy to remove some benign but irritating moles on a forty-four-year-old house-painter's back, and arthrocentesis—withdrawing and analysing the fluid—of a sixty-eight-year-old retired man's knee joint.

By lunchtime—three-quarters of an hour later than it should have been—she had seen twenty-seven patients, some of whom she had been forced to despatch far more quickly than she was happy with.

Now Mrs Mayberry appeared—with coffee.

'Thanks *very* much, Mrs Mayberry,' Francesca said to her brightly, 'but I won't have coffee in my lunch-break in future. Do just bring me the one cup at four. For now, I'm just going to grab a sandwich in the kitchen so I can hit the ground running fifteen minutes from now when it all starts again.'

'Dr Brady always skipped lunch when he ran this late,' Mrs Mayberry said, sweetly firm. 'He said coffee kept him going, and then if there was a slack period in the afternoon I'd slip him in a banana or a piece of cake. Your mother always made sure to leave him something when she went off to her committees.'

'Yes, she bakes wonderful cakes, doesn't she?' Francesca said. 'I won't be nearly so spoiled as Dad was.'

Mrs Mayberry laid the coffee cup on Francesca's desk. 'Sharon Baron has come early for her appointment, I'm afraid,' she said with a little sigh. 'She's been waiting ten minutes already. And I squeezed someone else in at three.'

'In that case, the sandwich might have to wait, I guess, and I'll see Mrs Baron—'

'Miss Baron.'

'I'll see Miss Baron now.'

'Dixie will show her into the pink room,' Mrs Mayberry replied.

Five minutes later Francesca entered the pink room herself through the communicating door between it and the office. She left the coffee cooling on her desk, as she really didn't want it.

'And I must give you my congratulations!' she said, after an initial greeting to the very large woman who sat uncomfortably on the examining table.

'On what?' Two already small eyes were narrowed further in suspicion.

'On your new nephew.' Even without the sing-song names and Preston Stock's briefing, it would have been obvious that Caron and Sharon were sisters. The resemblance was unmistakable. But the beaming smile which had softened Caron's coarse face at the sight of 'Dr Luke' on

Saturday was not hinted at anywhere in this woman's very similar features.

'So she's had the baby, has she? As if I care!'

'I'm sorry?'

'Caron and I don't speak. She's not coming to you now, is she?' Again the puffy skin around her eyes had creased in suspicion.

'No, she sees Dr Wilde, but there was a bit of an emergency on Saturday with the baby and I ended up being involved in her delivery.' She didn't want to say too much because if the two sisters were at odds then confidentiality became an issue.

Sharon Baron grunted, and said no more.

End of subject, evidently...which was probably for the best, given the number of patients she had to get through today. She said briskly, 'What's brought you to see me today, then, Miss Baron?'

'Well, it's my dyer-beat-us again, of course.'

Diabetes. It fitted. She looked at the chart. Adult onset. Chronically out of control. Weight loss would definitely help. Oral hypoglycaemics evidently didn't adequately, although in theory they should. The idea of injecting insulin had been rejected wholesale more than once by the patient, however.

'This testing my pee that Dr Stock got me on,' Sharon was grumbling now. 'What's it doing for me? I fiddle around with it and it's a big fat nuisance, and then I'm just supposed to lose weight. I *can't* lose weight. It's my glands and my hediterry.'

'Your what?'

'My hediterry. Mom was fat, Dad was fat.'

Francesca controlled a sigh, then she remembered Luke's throw-away line the other day that he'd done a year and a half's training in endocrinology—the study of glandular diseases. That encompassed diabetes so it wouldn't be malicious of her to suggest a visit to her rival.

Yes, it would! Sharon wouldn't benefit from a whole fleet of diabetic specialists because her problem was in compliance, not diagnosis or symptoms.

On the other hand, though, since a patient's own involvement was so important in the management of diabetes, perhaps Luke had some extra insight into how Miss Baron's compliance could be improved. She hesitated for another few seconds, then decided. Sharon was receiving some form of disability pension so there'd be some payment forthcoming, and by the sound of things Luke needed all the income he could get, if he was reduced to bartering medical services for carpentry on his porch. The sound of hammers and saws had rung and screamed in the air for hours yesterday afternoon.

It wasn't the best reason in the world to refer a patient elsewhere, but…

'Have you ever been to see Dr Wilde about any of this?' she suggested politely, cutting off a rambling complaint that seemed to involve everything from bunions to the government. In mentioning Luke, she still couldn't even decide—was she generously doing him a favour because she wanted to support him, or maliciously sending him an impossible patient?

It was soon evident that the question was irrelevant.

Sharon's virulent flow was redirected at once at the mention of his name. 'Luke Wilde?' she screeched indignantly. 'I'd die before I'd go to him. He's a drug fiend! His father killed my sister!'

'Your sister? *Caron*?' Once again, Francesca was shocked and confused. To have the accusation of fatal malpractice come up for the second time in the space of a few hours…

'No, not Caron!' Sharon said impatiently. 'My other sister. Pastille.'

'Pas—?'

'Pastille,' Sharon repeated. 'It's unusual, isn't it? And

pretty. She was the youngest, and Ma couldn't think of any more rhymed names so she picked that. Sweet. Makes you think of candy. She *was* sweet, too, till that rat got her into trouble. Only eighteen, and Dr Wilde made her die having that baby.'

'Now, there's absolutely no proof, is there, that—?'

'Caron's crazy to go to him,' Sharon announced, waving Francesca's careful caveat aside.

'She goes to Luke Wilde, not the old doctor—not Luke's father.' Again, it was a fight to stick to the facts and to sort them out from the confusing mess of rumour and the equating of James Wilde's medical practice with that of his son.

Sharon shrugged. 'They're both the same. Should lose their licences. Come on! He should, shoudn't he?'

'I thought he *had* lost his licence.' Surely that was what her father had said, or what he'd implied.

'No! I called the police on him for killing my sister but they didn't do nothing about it,' Sharon countered indignantly.

'Then that proves it, surely,' Francesca said, with more confidence than she felt. This was going nowhere, and she wasn't going to form any conclusion about Luke Wilde in the midst of this sea of accusation.

She went on even more firmly, 'I'm sorry, Sharon, but it's inappropriate for me to be talking about a fellow doctor in these terms and to be listening to you talking this way. Dr Wilde—Dr *Luke* Wilde—is extremely well respected down at Wayans Falls Hospital.' This fact had been immediately apparent to her on Saturday, and was so far one of the few real points in Luke's favour.

'I've heard no reliable reports of wrong-doing by either him or his father.' Which means I've just dismissed Mrs Mayberry as *un*reliable, she realised parenthetically. 'Until I do—*unless* I do—I'm not going to criticise him or come out against him in any way. What's more, I'll continue to send him any patients whom I feel could benefit from his particular areas of expertise,' she finished expansively, as if she'd already sent him a dozen such patients.

'Well, *I'm* not going to him,' Sharon muttered. 'And if you tell me there's no better pills you can give me to stop this sugar in my pee, or whatever, then I'll get on my way. I've got things to do.'

She left in a hostile huff.

Francesca went back through her office to pick up the next patient's chart a little shakily, before heading through into the blue room on the opposite side. It worked quite well, shuttling to and fro like this as she worked her way through the pile of charts on her desk. Actual surgical procedures were done in a third room across the corridor, but she only had one of those scheduled for today—a fine needle breast biopsy arranged last week by Preston Stock.

The one mildly irritating feature of the set-up was that it seemed to please Mrs Mayberry's sense of what was fitting to alternate male and female patients when she could so that women were sent to the pink room and men to the blue. Francesca found this rather too cute for her taste, and it didn't always work either as women tended to outnumber men by virtue of their reproductive systems, and perhaps their tendency to keep going for their children's sakes until they were really ill, when they should have taken to their beds days earlier.

With a vague sense of reluctance, she decided she'd better mention her problem with the 'pink for girls and blue for boys' system to Mrs Mayberry fairly soon. Definitely not now, though.

She picked up the next chart and was about to head into the blue room when Mrs Mayberry herself appeared. 'I'm *so* sorry about that awful woman!' she said in a breathless, conspiratorial whisper. She hadn't knocked. 'I've *tried* to fob her off, truly I have, by saying we don't have any appointments available, but she won't *be* fobbed. Of course she's the sort of patient that the Wilde practice should be seeing, but she won't realise it.'

'The Wilde practice? Because of her diabetes?'

'No, because she's on disability, I meant. His practice accepts all those types. The welfare people. And he ought to realise that because it's the only way he'll be able to keep patients. Isn't it? With him taking the welfare types?'

While I take the respectable patients with good health insurance? Francesca wondered inwardly. Like pink for girls and blue for boys? 'He won't make much of a living that way,' she suggested drily aloud. She was finding this very difficult, but felt she had to contain and conceal her anger.

'Oh, but *they're* always better off than the decent people who work hard at a job all day,' Mrs Mayberry said.

'Well, Mr Jaeger is waiting,' Francesca said pleasantly.

'Yes, of course.' Mrs Mayberry disappeared again. She hadn't taken the coffee.

At four o'clock it was still there, quite cold now, and although she was not remotely tempted to drink it its aroma was just strong enough and attractive enough to remind Francesca that it had got to the point where she really would like a fresh cup. No cup was forthcoming, however, although at four-thirty there had appeared, while she was doing the breast biopsy, a large slice of cheap cake and a glass of water.

It was at this point that Francesca began to reach the rather depressing realisation that Mrs Mayberry was going to be a problem.

Dixie Andrews wasn't. Dixie was delightful! 'Forty-seven down and three to go-o,' she sang in a doom-laden monotone as she slipped into Francesca's office just after the latter's discovery of the cake.

'You keep a count?' Francesca asked in disbelief.

'Only on bad days.'

'And is this a bad day? Tell me, Dixie, because I really

want to know.' Twenty-five-year-old Dixie had been with the practice for a year.

'Girlfriend,' she replied slangily, 'it's your first day—of course it's a bad one!'

'Good!'

'Because that means it'll get better?'

'That means it'll get better,' Francesca agreed fervently. 'I was in a big group practice for my residency. There was always someone else to take the slack or, if there wasn't, at least there were other people to complain to!'

'You should consider a partnership, Dr Brady,' Dixie suggested frankly.

'I may do that,' she answered. Then, because she wanted to be cautious at this stage, she added, 'I'm going to consider a lot of options, in fact, although I'm certainly not going to make any changes too hastily.'

'Wise idea. Wait till Betty steps down from the throne,' Dixie agreed, and her tone was so guileless that Francesca wasn't even convinced it had been meant as a dig.

Now Dixie was holding out the chart she'd picked up from Francesca's desk. 'Mr Saltman,' she said. 'He seems quite upset. Thought you'd want to know. We see his wife usually. She's pregnant at the moment and on full home bed-rest because of pre-term labour. Don't know if that's what's bothering him today. He certainly doesn't look great.'

'His wife's not with him?'

'No, so maybe it's nothing to do with her. But when they're upset I like to let you know. I always used to let your dad know, especially when it's a nice guy like Eric Saltman. Did I do the right thing?'

'Yes, Dixie, thanks,' she said, and took the chart from the nurse.

'I took his blood pressure, temp and pulse. It's written down. His heart rate's pretty high. And his hands were so warm and sweaty. He was trembling a bit, too. I—I really hope there's nothing badly wrong.'

'We'll soon see,' Francesca promised.

Going in to Eric Saltman, it didn't take her long to reach a tentative diagnosis. He was upset, and upset about the fact that he was upset, too. He was a tall man, forty years of age, with slightly greying hair and an intelligent face that was still handsome despite a degree of pouchiness and eyes that were a little too prominent.

'I don't understand why I'm feeling like this,' was his first response to her question about why he'd come. 'I thought at first it was Gina. My wife.'

'I know,' Francesca smiled. 'Due in a bit over two months, isn't she? I bet you'll be glad when the bed-rest is over!'

'I sure will! It's been a strain for both of us, and at first I thought that was the only problem. Now, though…' He shook his head. 'It's got to be more than that! I'm having palpitations. I can't walk down to our mailbox and back without getting breathless and feeling my thighs burn.'

He outlined a few more symptoms, each of which added greater certainty to Francesca's suspicions. An examination completed the picture within minutes—a thyroid gland which was enlarged, smooth and rather soft, rapid heartbeat and the trembling that Dixie had commented on. Also, his eyelids were retracted and the nails on several of his fingers were separating from their beds.

It all suggested hyperthyroidism fairly clearly, but tests would have to be done to determine what type and, therefore, what treatment was needed. She told him all this, fairly confident that she'd pitched it all at the right level of complexity, clarity and reassurance. He was a professional man who worked from an office in his mountain hide-away home, creating and mailing out three business newsletters to very specialised niche markets, he had told her, and he seemed to respond well to what she had said.

'I knew it was something,' he said, after taking it all in. 'It's not life-threatening, you say?'

'No, nor should it restrict your future in any way. But we do need to do some tests.'

'Which can be done here?'

'Well, the first one, yes, but then a specialist attached to a hospital—'

'Because, with Gina on bed-rest, I just don't want to be gone that long. It's over an hour round trip to Wayans Falls from our place, and we're out of the way. If she suddenly had a problem…'

This was when it occurred to Francesca that here was a patient whom she really ought to send to Luke. The thought of him had been nagging at the back of her mind all day, and the more she considered it the less she could believe what she'd heard. Mrs Mayberry had undoubtedly been listening to too much gossip, and Sharon Baron clearly had too many problems and prejudices of her own to be reliable on the subject.

But it did make sense of Luke's situation. He was battling that most sinister of enemies—scandal—and it was going to be a tough fight. People believed that his father had been criminally negligent, and some also believed that Luke himself was involved. Whatever she herself came to believe when she knew the full facts, she was going to give him the benefit of the doubt quite scrupulously now.

It's why he's come back, she realised. He's fighting to clear his father's name and his own reputation, too. That's courageous, and suggests integrity. He could so easily just have walked away, practised in some other part of the country and no one in his new life would ever have known. But that wasn't good enough for him. All this time the Brady practice has been humming along without a single stain, idling like a well-tuned machine ready for me to take over. It's no wonder, perhaps, that he's bitter, that he resents me. If I could show him that I'm on his side, and show the town that I'm on his side, by sending Eric Saltman to him...

Then what? She didn't really think through just what she was hoping for. All she was sure of was that she did not want this hostility between herself and a fellow doctor to continue. She'd never worked that way. During training and practice thus far, she'd always got much further with co-operation than competition.

'A specialist would be best, Mr Saltman,' she told her anxious patient now, 'but I understand your problem with that. There may be another option.'

'Yes?' He sounded eager, which was good, but she was nervous about saying it all the same, still threaded through with reluctance.

'Luke Wilde has much more experience with endocrine disorders than I do. If he could organise the tests for you, and do them in his office...'

'That'd be great!' Eric Saltman's green eyes lit up, un-clouded by any doubt. Either he didn't believe the rumours or he hadn't heard them.

She asked casually, 'How long have you lived up here, Mr Saltman?'

'Just on a year. We were Manhattanites before that, but we realised we hated the city and that we could both work just as well up here. My wife writes children's books. Why, would it have been better for me now if we'd stayed? Better care in the city?'

'Oh, no, nothing like that,' she said quickly. 'Luke Wilde is extremely good.' If my own judgement is all I go by. 'I just wondered, that's all. Nice to know a bit about my patients.'

She smiled at him and his brow cleared. 'Oh. Right. Yes. And Dr Wilde is good, is he? In that case, please do...what? Write me a referral letter to give him?'

'Better than that. I'll speak to him personally and get

him to give you a call,' she said, throwing caution to the winds.

Had Luke given her the remotest encouragement to think he'd even listen to what she had to say?

What you don't realise, Luke Wilde, she threatened silently to his image, so clear in her mind's eye, is that I'm as stubborn as you seem to be, and possibly far more principled!

CHAPTER FOUR

'MRS MAYBERRY, you didn't get a chance to bring me that coffee at four,' Francesca said to her secretary at a little after five when the last patient of the day had gone.

'Oh, I'm sorry, honey. I thought you could drink the cup I made you at lunch. It was still sitting on your desk,' she responded sweetly yet firmly.

'Well, I'm not very keen on cold coffee,' Francesca said mildly. 'Tomorrow, let's skip the cup at lunch and keep the one at four.'

'You won't sleep!' Mrs Mayberry threatened kindly, 'drinking it that late in the day.'

'Oh, I don't think it'll be a problem.'

Mrs Mayberry didn't reply.

Francesca suppressed a sigh. Her shoulders ached. And her neck. Her head, too, if she really thought about it. And what was that odd feeling in her stomach?

Hunger. She'd missed lunch completely, and had found the wedge of cheap supermarket cake so unappetising she'd only eaten two mouthfuls. She remembered enough of the Brady practice routine—and clearly it hadn't changed one iota in twenty-five years—to know that Mrs Mayberry always let herself out the side door after tidying up, which meant that she herself was now free to go through to the kitchen and make the sandwich she so badly needed. Dinner later would be easy, as she'd anticipated stress in these first days and had laid in a good stock of microwave meals.

Ten minutes later, a sandwich and a glass of juice in hand, she went out into the late afternoon, craving fresh air. The old swing seat still hung beneath the big oak tree in the garden, kept—like everything else—in good repair. She rocked lazily for several minutes, polishing off her sandwich in record time, then heard the sound of hammering start up again along the street.

Luke was working on his porch again. She hadn't heard the sound all day so perhaps he'd had patients. Or perhaps she'd just been too busy and too thoroughly closeted inside to hear the ringing sound. It was perfectly possible under the circumstances, which she now knew so much more about, that he hadn't had any patients at all.

Impulsively she jumped off the swing and headed for the back lane. She'd go down there right now while her impetus and her determination were still fresh. After all, hadn't she told Eric Saltman not half an hour ago that she would talk to Luke personally about his case? If she got her head bitten off, at least she'd know she'd done the right thing, and with any luck might have managed to get in a few bites of her own in return!

It might have been sensible to change first. She was wearing the low but smart heeled black pumps, pale grey wool trousers with a cherry and grey silk blouse that had seemed appropriately efficient and pretty for her first day—the shoes, in particular, weren't very suitable for a rutted and grassy back lane. It was too late now. She was halfway there.

The new porch looked great. Still hammering, and with his back to her, Luke didn't notice Francesca's approach so she stood there for a good minute or more, watching him at work, trying to muster her feelings—trying to decide what her feelings *were*. Anger? Definitely! Pity? Somehow Luke Wilde wasn't a man you could pity for long.

The work was nearly finished, and a pale expanse of smooth, freshly cut pine now stretched across a space where two days ago there had been only sagging and half-rotten old boards. Luke was hammering the last three lengths of wood into place now. Already cut to the right size, they were slotted in and just needed to be nailed to the supporting beams below.

He was adept at the job and held several nails in readiness between his teeth, positioning one perfectly straight and giving a light tap to anchor it in place before driving it all the way in with three or four accurate and sweetly timed blows of the big hammer.

She couldn't bear to interrupt. He was so close to being finished. Just six more nails. If she hailed him now he'd stop work and she'd rob him of the sense of satisfaction in having that last nail down. So she waited. And watched, of course, still struggling in a mire of much too complex feelings.

He was wearing those jeans again. There was a split in the worn fabric across the top of the left thigh at the back, and when he moved it gaped open to reveal a slash of olive skin lightly dappled with dark hair. The day was warm enough and the work strenuous enough that there was a faint sheen of sweat on the back of his neck, and the wavy tendrils of walnut-brown hair that fell there against his fine skin were slightly damp, too.

She felt an odd tingling and a breathlessness that didn't come from any exertion, and had the sudden and extremely disturbing understanding that despite their angry exchanges of the past couple of days she wanted him, physically, in exactly the way she had wanted him as a teenager.

Then she had known so little about life and about herself that she'd got it all naïvely mixed up with a fifteen-year-old's notions of love, but now she recognised it for what it really was—pure, simple lust. She wanted Luke Wilde's strong body against hers with a primitive physical desire that was at once intoxicating, overpowering and appalling. She wanted his mouth to rove over her skin, his passion-driven breathing hammering against her breasts, and she wanted to spread her fingers, as she had done so clumsily at fifteen, and muss them through his hair—damn him!

Surely it wasn't possible! Surely these things didn't last for fifteen years! Somehow, though, it had—lying dormant in some part of her, quite forgotten until these past few days when she'd so unexpectedly encountered him again.

And not just 'encountered' either. He was in her life now, living just a few doors from her, and he wasn't going to go away. Which meant that she would *have* to master this!

It ought to be possible. She had a bright mind, and in the relationships she'd had since leaving Darrensberg for college it had always been her mind that had called the shots. This time, though…

Whack! The last nail was knocked into place, the hammer-blow ringing in the air afterwards for several seconds like an echo. She let out a controlled sigh, and only then realised that she'd been holding her breath all during those final blows.

He turned to drop the hammer onto his canvas tool pouch and his dry drawled greeting told her that he must have known she was there all along. Why hadn't he given a sign of it?

'Hi,' she murmured ineptly, as if she were still fifteen and still paralysed in his presence. As if she was fifteen and had told him yesterday that she loved him, instead of being thirty and confessing to an ancient crush.

Which was ridiculous and impossible, and she wouldn't put up with such foolishness in herself, so she added quickly and far more smoothly, 'You've finished. It looks good.'

'It does, doesn't it?' he agreed neutrally. 'I don't think I'll paint or stain it. I'll just put on several coats of that tough polyurethane so it'll look pale and cool and clean.'

'It'll be nice. Then are you going to…?' She glanced upwards and around hesitantly. There was still so much to be done!

'Fix the trim, replace the split boards and broken slates

and paint the place?' he guessed. 'Yes, eventually. When I
get the…uh…time.' And the money. He didn't add this,
but they both knew it was part of the equation.

'What colours?' Keep talking. Skip over the awkward-
ness. Stick to her scrupulous determination to play fair.

'Something traditional, I think,' he said, not looking at
her and scowling a little in an absent-minded way. 'White,
with a really dark forest green.' Now he looked up and
smiled crookedly. 'I did get some suggestions and an es-
timate from an artistically inclined house-painter, but his
concept didn't appeal. The colours he proposed were sage,
heather and celadon. Didn't sound like paint at all. Sounded
more like what movie stars are calling their children.'

She laughed and relaxed just a little, while privately
wondering if celadon was that rather weird pale green that
the trim around the eaves of her place was painted in. To
be honest, she wasn't entirely sure about the Brady Family
Practice Center's new paint job. It was a little too elaborate,
and would probably look out of date well before it weathered.

She said, half to herself, 'Yes, I quite like the traditional
colours, too.'

'You didn't choose your current ones, then?'

'No, Dad had it all done before his illness.'

There was a silence. Then he said, 'Sorry about your
dad.'

'Yes. He almost died, and he'll never be very strong
again now.'

'It must have been hard, for a man so ambitious, to face
giving up work.'

'It was. If I hadn't been taking over…'

'It was what he always wanted for you.'

'Well, no, I think that was quite a recent idea.'

'Hmm.' He shrugged, almost as if he didn't believe her
and as if her correction had grated somehow.

'But your…your dad, Luke, and your mom. Are they

retired somewhere now?' she hazarded, determined to hang onto the small softening between them since it was clearly so tenuous.

'Not exactly.' Again it was brief, a little too off-hand. 'Dad died two years ago.'

'Oh, I'm sorry.'

'Yes.' He nodded, strain and sadness in his face. Anger, too. 'It was cancer. He was ill for a while. He kept practising as long as he could, but he only had a handful of patients left when he finally called it quits. Mom had a hard time. She needed to get out of Darrensberg. She's doing a lot better now, living with my brother, Adam, and his family in Boston. She's crazy about her grandchildren.'

'And Adam is doing well?'

'Oh, yes. Rising fast in his father-in-law's firm.'

He turned and began to gather some stray nails from the new porch, saying nothing more.

There were some missing links in the story. They almost shouted at Francesca but she didn't dare to bring them up in case it broke the mood. Nor did she dare, yet, to bring up the question of Eric Saltman and the tests he needed. Seeing Luke again, seeing the hard energy and determination in his face and still the bitterness, she remembered just how hostile he'd been on Saturday at the suggestion of any professional link between them.

She almost decided to go. Perhaps a phone call or a note about Eric Saltman would be more businesslike.

'Well…' she began, searching for a credible parting line, but before she could find one Luke closed his eyes for a moment and gave a gusty sigh.

'I'm going to have a beer,' he said gruffly. 'Would you like one?'

'Um, sure.' And there it was again, the feeling of being fifteen and on Cloud Nine.

'Out here?'

'That'd be nice,' she agreed. 'I've been inside all day.'

She rubbed at her neck. 'I had—' Fifty patients. She stopped just in time. 'Some settling in to do.'

It was not very convincing, perhaps, but it was the best she could come up with. She smiled at him to punctuate the line, but he had already leapt gracefully up onto the porch and disappeared inside the front door. He returned just a minute later with two light, lo-cal beers and tossed one to her.

She fumbled but held the catch, and he invited her to sit down.

So she did, like he had, on the new porch. The wood smelled fresh and fragrant and clean, and if she was getting sawdust and splinters on her fairly expensive wool pants she suddenly didn't care. There was something about this—a quiescence in their hitherto stormy dealings that satisfied her hugely.

Was it just because, if this had happened to her at fifteen, she'd have thought she'd died and gone to heaven? Surely not! She frowned, pulled the ring of the drink can and took a swig. She only drank beer occasionally and didn't like it all that much, but this one was light and pleasant, not the sort of full-bodied beer she'd have expected him to favour, and she was starting to feel surprisingly relaxed.

He was watching her, she realised a minute later, and when she looked up at him he drawled teasingly, 'I didn't get around to mentioning this yesterday, Chess, but actually I was crazy about you, too.'

'*What*?'

'You heard. Crazy about you. Hey, it was fifteen years ago. If you can admit to it so can I.'

'No!'

He shrugged. 'I was.'

'But you were—you were— You never asked me out! You hardly came near me!'

'And when I did you ran like a rabbit. Callow youth that

I was, I interpreted this as dislike on your part. Or fear, even.'

'Well, yes,' she admitted shortly, 'I was certainly terrified of you.'

'And, weird though this may seem, I had difficulty in seeing terror as a *positive* response to me, Chess.'

'I told you yesterday, I was a teenage girl. I was overwhelmed. My response to you wasn't logical.'

'And I was a teenage boy. Also overwhelmed.' His lazy, rather wry smile was doing things to her, making her watch his lips and remember that kiss of theirs again. His lips hadn't changed either. They were still firm, well moulded, very masculine and very expressive.

'I guess you *were* a boy. Eighteen or so. Then you seemed very much a man to me. *Too* much so!'

'I was certainly trying to be!' He laughed. 'I showed off to you mightily, too, I seem to remember.'

'No, I wouldn't have forgotten that.'

'I did!' he insisted lightly. 'Don't you remember the night I lectured you at great length on the beat poets and Jack Kerouac?'

'Jack Kerouac! *On the Road*. I hung on every word you said!'

'And I sure said some! I seem to remember holding forth for a good half-hour.'

'But it was fascinating! I went out and tried to buy a copy of it as soon as I could wangle Mom into a trip down to Pioneer Mall. But bookstores in malls in upstate New York don't run to books like *On the Road*, I found. So I never read it and that felt like the bitter end.' She laughed, suddenly rather fond of her foolish youthful self. 'Because I'd rehearsed a whole *conversation* we were going to have about it in which I said something incredibly perceptive about—let's see—its evocative use of language, and you were going to look at me and suddenly see how bright and sensitive I was, and—'

'Chess, don't you know *anything* about teenage boys?' He parroted her own words of yesterday in a low, teasing growl. 'I didn't care about bright and sensitive then. You were *beautiful*, and when you listened to me, spouting on about the poetry and freedom of the road, that night with your big gray eyes all starry and swimming, I thought, 'Gee, this Kerouac stuff really works!' God, I was hot for you, I just *wanted* you. That's an admission, isn't it? Sorry.'

He winced and shook his dark head, making a recalcitrant lock of hair fall onto his forehead. 'It sounds so crass. Boys are crass at eighteen. You know, though, that it demeans me, not you. You were up on a pedestal, as far as I was concerned, and it was where you deserved to be, while I…I was this hot, writhing ball of lust who shouldn't have even *dared* to dream of you that way.'

'Oh, but I wanted you, too, Luke. *Badly*! Only I was too immature to know it. Until that time when you—'

'Kissed you, out in the garden. The moment came and I grabbed it. I *had* to. Or I think I would have exploded.'

'It felt like an explosion, so sudden and so wonderful. My heart was pounding.'

'When you actually responded I couldn't believe it. I was tingling all over, practically shaking.'

'And I was in heaven over it. Absolute heaven.'

'Yes,' he agreed, frowning now. 'Until you chickened out and went to—'

'Chickened out? You were the one who stopped it, Luke.' Tearing himself away when Mom called from the house.

He shrugged. 'We seem to remember this part differently.'

'It was a long time ago,' she pointed out, while thinking, But I'm right. I didn't chicken out. I'd have defied Mom and Dad totally to be with Luke if he'd showed that he wanted it—if he hadn't left town.

'It was,' Luke was saying heavily, 'a long time ago.'

There was a stiff little pause, a crack in the conversation which let regret pour in.

She hadn't intended to say half of that. Neither had he, surely! Things had got a little dangerous at some point which now made her original reason for this meeting, the case of Eric Saltman, suddenly seem much safer by comparison.

As a way of introducing the subject, she asked quickly, 'Um, how is Caron Baron doing? And the baby?'

'Great, actually,' he answered, examining a nail in the new porch. It wasn't quite all the way in. He picked up the hammer and gave it two quick blows. 'She'll be discharged tomorrow. I drove down to see her first thing this morning.'

'What's she going to call him?'

'You say that with a degree of trepidation.'

'And is it justified?'

'Uh, yes, well, I have to admit. She's decided on Norad.'

'Ooh!'

'It's her brother, Daron, spelled backwards. She and Daron are close so it's nice, really, and he'll be just tickled to death. He's mildly retarded. Great guy. Very warm. He lives with Caron and her boyfriend up off a back road in the woods in a pretty dreadful mobile home, but at heart they're good people and they'll manage.'

'No abuse?'

'No abuse,' he said firmly.

'That's good.' But she was thinking more about something else. A mobile home in the woods. The same place where, according to Betty Mayberry and Caron's own sister, Sharon, another sister had died fifteen years ago, giving birth to Luke's child?

Sitting here with him in the late sunshine and sipping cold beer on this beautifully made new porch, it seemed even more impossible than it had seemed in her office. Had he ever been that wild? Wild—it wasn't even the right word for something that sordid. He *had* been wild, certainly. She remembered this herself very clearly.

He had driven far too fast sometimes. He hadn't finished school. And he'd just ridden off out of town on that bike of his quite shortly after their kiss and, to all intents and purposes, never been seen again. Those were the facts. This sordid story wasn't. To her—yet. And there was nastiness in it somewhere, either in what had happened or in the minds of the people who had spread the story when it wasn't true.

Impulsively she said, 'I met Sharon Baron today.'

'Oh, yes?' Immediately his expression was shuttered.

'She has type two diabetes, very badly controlled. Really, it would make more sense for her to see you.'

'She'll never do that. Not while Caron and Daron—and Norad—are my patients.'

'I gathered that.'

She waited for him to come up with more but he didn't, just sat there drinking his beer and staring up at the fractured wooden porch trim as if calculating how he'd repair and restore it.

But she was stubbornly determined to get through to him. It made too much sense professionally for her to baulk at it for personal reasons. She said, firmly matter-of-fact, 'One patient I do want to hand over to you, though, is a man called Eric Saltman, who shows all the signs of some form of hyperthyroid condition. I remembered what you'd said about having trained a little in that area, and it seemed more practical to—'

'No. Absolutely not,' he cut in.

OK, she'd been expecting this so she wasn't going to back out of the confrontation now.

'But *why*, Luke?'

The cautious truce between them, with its pleasant aura of relaxation overlying the slightly dangerous undercurrent of awareness, was gone now. He had tensed at once, put down his beer and slid off the porch, no longer lazily rest-ing one leg on the new planking and swinging the other off the edge but prowling on the short, vibrantly green grass.

She was instantly angry, too. '*Why*?' she repeated. 'I had fifty patients today. I was swamped. I don't know what the town has against you that you're struggling like this. I've heard some rumours, but I've taken them with a pinch of salt.'

'Have you, now?'

'Yes! I have!'

'I wonder why,' he said on an odd note.

Because I was starry-eyed about you at fifteen, Luke Wilde, and unfortunately for some weird reason it hasn't gone away. She didn't say it, of course, but she felt it, in every pulse and every nerve ending, which made her say very pompously, 'Because it seemed the fair thing to do. I don't think of myself as someone who makes snap judge-ments.'

He looked at her cynically. 'That's very noble of you.'

Perhaps she couldn't blame him for the sneer. It had been a horribly prim statement.

'Perhaps noble motives are an alien idea to you, Luke,' she retorted dismissively, 'but the point is that *you* need patients and *I* need to offload, and surely if I give you the benefit of the doubt then the town will start to as well.'

'Why? Because good little Miss Chessie Brady wouldn't ever support anyone who was nasty and bad?' he jeered tightly. 'And because the successful Dr Brady that little Miss Chessie has now miraculously become wouldn't sully her own professional reputation by any association with a reprobate doctor?'

'Yes! You can put it that way if you like, but yes! What's wrong with that, Luke? A professional and personal show of support until you prove yourself, which, of course, I hope you will.'

That prim tone again. His eyes were blazing, and somehow their fire was undermining her anger, distracting her, making her angry at herself instead.

'Because it's damned condescending,' he flared out now. 'I'm a very stubborn man, Dr Brady.'

That makes two of us.

'I don't like to run away from failure,' he went on. 'I like to look it right in the face and turn it into success. It's why I came back here. But if I can't make it, can't restore the Wilde practice's reputation in this town without the help of Dr Francesca Brady, of all people, then I *will* run away! I'll call it quits and get out!… Which is, perhaps, what you'd better do now, Francesca, before I say something I'll regret.'

'Luke, please…' She slid from the porch, too, and came towards him, angry—*very* angry—but desperately wanting to get past this and force him to get past it, too.

He froze and scowled down at her and she laid her hand on his bare forearm instinctively, a gesture that wordlessly begged him to tell her more. There was *so* much he wasn't saying. She could feel it in the air between them, as heavy as the scent of the ancient, untidy lilacs that had just begun to bloom in this neglected garden.

He looked down at her hand on his arm and she followed his gaze, and suddenly it was as if an electric current had been switched on. His hand twisted and moved to grip her forearm as she was gripping his, locking them together all along that ten or twelve inches of sensitive inner skin.

The contact wasn't nearly enough. She wanted more of it, and so did he. The evidence was there in his breathing, ragged now, and in his stillness. She lifted her other hand to his shoulder and rested it there as she looked up at him mutely, not knowing what to say, not wanting to say anything, only wanting to feel this and reach him so that *he* could talk.

'No, Chess,' he said, his face scored with tight lines of control. 'You can't get to me this way.'

He slid his hand up past her elbow, creasing her silk blouse with the heat from his palms, and matched the movement with his other hand so that he was gripping her tightly now. His thighs were pressed hard against hers, and his hips, too. She could feel his arousal and it melted her, made her swell with the impossible ecstasy of wanting him.

'I'm not going to do it. I'm not going to take you in my arms and put my mouth over yours and whisper a promise in your ear that we'll get through this together. We're not teenagers any more.'

'I know that...'

'Look at us! We're both on fire, aren't we?'

'Y-yes.' Her heart was racing madly, almost against his chest. She wanted to tangle her legs in his, bury her face in his neck, drink the taste of him.

'But I'm not going to do it, Chess. I'm not going to kiss you. *We're not on the same side*. And you're the last person in the world I need to do me any favours. I've already paid enough for this insane magnetism. I won't take this patient of yours. Deal with Eric Saltman yourself, Francesca, and get on with running your practice. I'll make my practice work despite you, not because of you, and this little matter...'

His thighs grazed hers deliberately and he pulled her even closer. It was a rough gesture, though, containing no tenderness, as if he was daring her to respond—to try and push him over the brink. There was nothing in his face that resembled the prelude to a kiss. 'It can be consigned to the past, where it belongs,' he finished.

Then he let her go and stepped back so abruptly that she almost fell forward, and she made a clumsy step as she steadied herself. No strong male hand shot out to shore her up. He simply watched, narrow-eyed, as if to stress that she was on her own.

'I don't understand you, Luke,' she said tightly. 'It was so nice just now when we were talking on the porch. I-I'm not your enemy. I don't want to be!'

'Perhaps you don't. But I'm on my own, Chess, and that's all there is to it. Now, go, OK, before we do something we'll both regret.'

Like sleeping together. That was what he meant. She could easily have done it, too. She was still throbbing, on fire, swamped by the strength of what he aroused in her. No one she had been involved with over the past twelve years had done this to her. None of them had even come close, and all she could come up with as an explanation was the hazy and decidedly non-medical theory that somehow her senses had locked onto him in her teens. No, it was ridiculous. That didn't happen to people. It was nonsense.

The fact remained, though, that she could have slept with him as easily as she'd have drunk a glass of water to slake her thirst on a hot day. Her body was crying out for it, and if he weren't presenting this iron wall of determination to resist...

Belatedly, she nodded. 'Yes, I'll go. And I'll send Eric Saltman to Wayans Falls if his initial blood test shows the need for follow-up that's more sophisticated than I can do myself.'

'And isn't that only what I'd do if you sent him to me?'

'I was hoping to avoid sending him down, that's all. He doesn't want to go.' She explained briefly about Gina Saltman's bed-rest. 'I thought with your greater knowledge of the field you might have been able to save him the trip.'

'I doubt it. You'll do a blood test for measurement of thyroid hormone secretion. It'll probably be high. You'll then give him a dose of radioactive iodide and send him down to Wayans Falls the next day to have the uptake measured, at which point Steve Kagan, who I'd thoroughly recommend, will take over in order to determine and carry out the most appropriate form of treatment. There's really no way to avoid him going to Wayans Falls, unless he decides to delay treatment until his wife's had the baby, which I wouldn't recommend if she's got another two months to go.'

'No,' she agreed. 'I wouldn't recommend it either.'

He spread his hands, as if to say, There you are, then, and with a feeling of failure and messiness about the whole exchange, she mumbled a few brief words and left.

Luke put away his tools, unable to dismiss the scene as he wanted to do and unable to credit that Dr Francesca Brady was really what she seemed—competent, professional and eager to build a working association of mutual respect. She seemed to trust him, but he had a very large parcel of complex past—in this town and elsewhere. How much did she know of that? How much did she believe? And how close was she to her father these days?

He might be weakened by illness now, but Frank Brady had once been a very strong-willed and complex man—a good husband and father, yes, but controlling, ambitious and self-righteous in his professional life, and prepared to go to the ends of the earth to protect the interests of those he loved.

Witness that particularly brutal scene fifteen years ago in the man's study—the very study where Chess had now no doubt begun to unpack her books.

Luke had always assumed that Chess had engineered that scene. If he'd thought otherwise then he wouldn't have left town, no matter what threats Frank Brady had made. Today, though, she seemed to have forgotten that part of the story.

He wondered again what she knew. She wasn't naïve, not any more, but she had been then. And since? Had she been kept at a distance? Perhaps she really didn't know the truth about her father's machinations.

Hell, though, why did it even matter? He had known

from the moment he decided to come back to Darrensberg that it would be his fight and his alone, and he wondered for the hundredth time just why it was of such importance to him to do this. He could have made a success in his profession elsewhere in the country with only a fraction of the effort.

Was it purely his pride and stubbornness? Purely a question of the Wilde family's honour? Or did it, in fact, have far more to do with Francesca Brady than he'd ever want to admit?

To hell with it! To hell with scandal, pride, introspection and women!

He was weary, sore and a blister had burst on his palm. And he was hungry, but couldn't eat yet. At certain times his body had more compelling needs than food.

He craved a shower, too. Steaming hot, maybe, to wash away the sweat and dirt from the heavy physical work he'd been doing. Or maybe icy cold, to wash away something that was a lot harder to get rid of than sweat—unsated arousal. In either case, though, the point was moot. He didn't have time for a shower just yet. Not yet. Not for another five long minutes, he knew.

He was already running just a crucial, painful half-hour late for one of his five times daily appointments with his most hated enemy—and most necessary friend—the hypodermic syringe.

Turning from the porch, he entered the house to keep the vital rendezvous.

CHAPTER FIVE

FRANCESCA didn't see Luke to speak to for some days. There was a considerable amount of deliberate avoidance, admittedly, but beyond that she was simply too swamped by patients and by the task of bringing the practice under her own control.

'Was Dr Stock this busy?' she asked Mrs Mayberry on Thursday morning, when the computer print-out of her day's appointments showed once again a relentless, non-stop schedule, with three hand-written additions squeezed in.

'No, he wasn't, because people were waiting for you, dear,' Mrs Mayberry said, depositing Francesca's morning coffee on her desk.

Her heart sank as she looked at it. The stuff arrived religiously at nine and at lunch, whether she drank it or not. It *didn't* arrive at four when she was desperate for it, and nothing she said or did made any difference. Short of completely blowing her stack at dear Betty, which she wasn't yet prepared to do because dear Betty had always been so good to her, she didn't know what more she could do.

Resigned, she reached for the rounded mug now and took an absent gulp. 'But people can't have been storing up things like flu or pregnancy.'

'Well, he sent most of the Ob/Gyns down to Dr Richards, the obstetrician in Stedman Point,' Mrs Mayberry explained. 'They'd known each other at medical school, and Dr Stock didn't feel very comfortable with Ob/Gyn work, he said.'

'Ah...' Francesca murmured.

That was a pity, since Ob/Gyn work remained both a

strength and an interest for her, and she'd now very possibly lost quite a number of such patients permanently to the unknown Dr Richards. Once again she wondered why Dad had suggested Preston Stock as a locum. She asked Mrs Mayberry about it. It seemed as good a time as any to do so, and if patients piled up a bit because she started a few minutes late, well, she was going to lose her lunch hour, anyway.

'Why Dr Stock?' was Mrs Mayberry's response. 'Oh, because he's Oliver Slade's grandson, of course. Dr Slade was your father's greatest inspiration at Harvard. If he hadn't died your father would have been where he belonged—in an Upper East Side practice in New York City.'

'Ah...' Francesca murmured again. 'OK.'

The explanation made little sense, other than confirming her perception that Dr Stock hadn't been remotely suitable for the position. Still, if she had lost a few Ob/Gyn patients, she clearly had plenty more. Scanning the appointment print-out, she saw four for today alone, although three of them were only annual pap smears. Perhaps if she kept sending them to Dr Richards in Stedman Point it would free up her schedule, make things less frantic.

But no! Because they were just the patients she wanted! Frustrated, she took another large gulp of the coffee. Aagh! It was so strong, and with far less milk than she liked. She hated having it sit here every morning, because it was hard not to drink it automatically—a kind of reflex, habitual action, like biting one's nails.

'Mrs Mayberry,' she said crisply, her anger rising. Dear Betty or not, she had to get through to the woman, take charge. 'I'm going to put some new guidelines into effect for you, and I expect them to be adhered to. First of all, we are *not* squeezing in extra patients who do not need urgent attention when the day's list is already crammed to the gills. You must either leave some slots vacant in a systematic way or send people elsewhere.'

'Elsewhere?' Mrs Mayberry echoed blankly, her mouth dropping open. 'You mean Stedman Point or Wayans Falls?'

'No, I do *not* mean that! I mean you must tell people to go to Luke Wilde.' Mrs Mayberry gasped, but Francesca ignored it and plunged on. 'Secondly, I don't want to work through lunch. You mustn't regard that as overflow time that can be regularly used to get through the backlog. I don't want to keep people waiting for half an hour after their scheduled appointments as our backlog builds during the morning, and by lunchtime I need the break to eat and to clear my head.

'I'll also be reviewing our overall schedule at the end of the week so I want you to be prepared for some changes there. It seems to me that we need some evening hours and some clear time for me to chase up test results or follow through by phone with certain specialists. And, finally, as I have now told you several times, I want coffee at four o'clock. I do not want it at nine or at lunch! Now, will you please ask Dixie to show Mr Pomeroy into the *pink* room.'

Mrs Mayberry fled wordlessly, and Francesca buried her face in her hands, feeling like an axe murderer. What had she done? Upset dear Betty! Dad would have been furious!

Couldn't I have handled it more tactfully? she scolded herself, her remorse making her forget the fact that she'd been trying to handle it tactfully all week.

She went into the pink room, but Mr Pomeroy wasn't there so she went back through her office and found him in the blue room, chafing at the varicose veins which she could see immediately must be giving him a lot of trouble. Some questions about general health and lifestyle revealed that he had been attempting to minimise the discomfort in a sensible way but without much result so she had to tell him that surgery was the next step. He seemed pleased at the idea.

Then, half an hour later, feeling very petty, she snatched

a moment to ask Dixie why Mr Pomeroy had been in the
blue room when she'd *specifically* asked for the pink.

'Mrs Mayberry didn't tell me that,' Dixie said, looking
a little askance, 'so I just did the usual and put him in the
blue. Sorry!'

'It's all right, Dixie. I was trying to make a point in rather
a silly way. It's not your fault—nor Mrs Mayberry's. I have
to say I'm planning to get rid of this his and hers colour
scheme as soon as I can, though!'

'Oh.'

Francesca looked a question.

'Mrs Mayberry loves it. It was her idea.'

'It's revolting,' Francesca snapped, realising she was
tired. People were supposed to sleep well in their childhood
room but she hadn't, despite her heavy days. She added
contritely, 'Is she upset?'

'She's sniffing.'

'And that means she's upset?'

'Dr Stock used to have her sniffing about six times a
week. It's not something to celebrate about, I'll say that.'

'But I had the impression she liked Dr Stock.'

'Well, she wouldn't have let on to you that she didn't,'
Dixie said. 'For your dad's sake. She's always been so loyal
to him.'

Now Francesca felt *really* bad. 'I'll have a talk with her
at lunchtime.' What lunchtime? 'We'll get everything
sorted out.'

When Francesca summoned Mrs Mayberry to her office
at one, foregoing her sandwich for the fourth day in a row,
things seemed to have gone beyond the point of sorting
out.

'It's just not going to work out,' Mrs Mayberry sobbed.
'I should have retired when Dr Brady did. I'm too set in
my ways to take to the change. I managed with Dr Stock
because I knew you'd soon be along and things would go
back to how they were. But now *you* have different ideas

and habits, too. You can't send your overflow patients to a drug addict. Your father had the highest possible standards about that sort of thing. And four o'clock is a *dreadful* time of day for coffee!'

'But what makes you so sure he's an addict, Mrs Mayberry?' Francesca questioned desperately. She knew the elderly receptionist was prone to gossip—and was starting to realise, as Dad evidently never had, what a liability this was in a medical practice—but this time she carried every nuance of conviction. 'Couldn't it be just rumour?'

'Rumour? Chessie, dear, I've seen it with my own eyes!' She was wiping those eyes with a tissue as she spoke, distracted now by indignation.

'Seen it? You mean seen him…high?'

'I've seen him stick a needle in his veins, that's what I've seen! It was two months ago, just a few weeks after he got the practice going again. I'd heard the stories already, of course. I had some mail for him, which had been delivered here by mistake, so I went down in my lunch break and there he was in his patients' bathroom with the door wide open and the needle in his hand. He didn't see me. I just put the mail down on the reception desk and left.

'He had his shirt lifted up and was pressing it into his side. Horrible! I suppose he has to use strange spots like that or all his veins would collapse. That's what they say about addicts, isn't it? I'm not completely naïve, Chessie, even though to you I seem so useless in this job.'

She began to sob again.

'I'm giving in my notice. Two weeks. Lyn Parker is looking for a job. I'll give you her number. I don't want to put you out. I just should have retired when Dr Stock took over, that's all.'

Francesca didn't try to argue because she decided it was probably the most sensible thing Mrs Mayberry had said all week. Transitions were hard. People *did* get set in their ways.

As for what Mrs Mayberry had seen Luke do, the graphic image burned in her mind, vivid, appalling, *believable*. Mrs Mayberry had seen it, yet…

Not Luke, she thought.

Why do I want to believe in him like this?

Not Luke. There must be another explanation, her mind insisted.

But she had to shove the subject forcefully from her thoughts in order to focus on what was at hand.

'Mrs Mayberry, I do understand how hard you've been trying,' she managed, and succeeded in concluding the difficult discussion with the right tactful words while making a mental note to herself to call Dad as soon as possible and tell him what had happened, then ask for his input on the question of a bonus cheque or a special parting gift.

Patients were already gathering in the waiting room when she ushered a somewhat more cheerful Mrs Mayberry out of the office, and she lifted her shoulder-length blonde hair and rubbed an aching neck. It looked like another long afternoon.

After work Francesca badly needed fresh air, food, too. She piled together a thick sandwich, grabbed a juice box, made sure her pager was in her pocket and her cellular phone in her bag and headed for the car. There was a look-out several miles out of town, north on Route 19, and it would be wonderful to sit up there for a while.

On her way up the street she glanced instinctively across at the Wilde place and Luke was there on his porch, laying down a coat of clear polyurethane with a large, thick brush. He was wearing those jeans again. He had the firm, sculpted physique of someone who ate properly and looked after his body well and the porch looked great, but both were lost to sight after another moment. They didn't disappear from her thoughts quite so easily.

She was tired, she realised again.

The look-out was beautiful and as soul-healing as she had remembered. She loved these mountains! Densely forested, dotted thickly with lakes, ponds and tumbling rivers, it was home to deer, black bear, beavers, raccoons—even a few rarely seen lynx. As a child, she had picked wild blueberries up here at the look-out and canoed along the Buckhorn River. She had swum in the fresh cold water of Weaver Lake and eaten barbecued ribs and hamburgers cooked on the public grills in the Darren County Recreation Park.

She climbed out of the car and ate her sandwich and drank her juice as she sat on the thick stone parapet that edged the look-out, trying to remember the names of the mountains that dreamed blue and untamed in the distance. Was that Mt Marcy to the left? And Saddleback Mountain? It didn't really matter. It was just beautiful.

In the fall, when the weather suddenly snapped cold, the leaves on all these trees flamed yellow and rust-brown, orange and crimson. People tried to get it on film but you really couldn't, not the sheer *quantity* of colour, the myriad variants of tone. It was wonderful to be back here, and to remember.

Then two large loud cars and a motorcycle arrived to provide her with another, less palatable memory. That's right. This was where teenagers came to park at dusk and beyond. After about nine on summer evenings a police car cruised up here regularly, and once or twice arrests had been made here for drinking or drugs.

Looking at the leather-clad biker, she suddenly thought of Luke and wondered if *he*'d ever been caught up here, doing something he shouldn't. Probably. Making out with some girl, if nothing worse.

I'll go, she thought. I don't want to stay here if those people are going to behave like louts.

She ate the last bite of her sandwich and jumped from the wall, meeting the biker, who grinned at her and said in a casual, friendly way, 'Cool, isn't it? The view? Man, you can *breathe*!' The two couples from the cars were very innocently setting out an evening picnic on the grass-surrounded picnic tables put there for the purpose.

Regaining her vehicle, Francesca reflected that it was a timely lesson—you shouldn't make assumptions, shouldn't judge by appearances.

Mrs Mayberry could have seen Luke giving himself a flu shot or a tetanus booster. She wouldn't put two and two together to make five!

'Let's talk about your test results in a moment, Mr Saltman,' Francesca prevaricated. 'You're obviously not well today. Is that what you've come about?'

'Yes,' he said with a nod. 'It's flu, I guess. I've had it for a couple of days, but today it's even worse. My temperature's over 104, and I feel...' He didn't finish, but he didn't need to. It was quite apparent that he felt *rotten*, and he'd arrived slumped in the back of a taxi.

'OK, let's take a look at you, then.'

She put her stethoscope to her ears, fumbling with it a little and wishing she had more time to think through what was going on. She had called Eric Saltman a week ago, the day after her confrontation with Luke on his new porch, and suggested he return to her for a blood test. She had come up with some story to explain Luke's non-involvement, which Mr Saltman hadn't questioned. He had come in on Thursday for the test, and today the results had come back.

She was on the point of calling him about it just after lunch—the news was good, on paper—and then she'd realised that he was on her list for this afternoon anyway, the last appointment of the day, so she hadn't made the call after all.

Truth to tell, the result had surprised her and she had wanted to buy time—not that the rest of her patients had given her much of that to spare. Eric Saltman's serum T4 level, which the blood test had measured, wasn't raised at all, and she had been so sure it would be because his symptoms were so classically indicative of an over-active thyroid.

Looking at him now, she'd have sworn you could write the textbook about him. Yet the test result was normal. The anomaly, on top of everything else, was unsettling her.

'Everything else' was not really so bad, perhaps. Just a continuation of her busy schedule, topped by the discovery that Lyn Parker, whom Mrs Mayberry had recommended to take over her job, was no longer available.

'I'm going to be working for Dr Wilde,' she had said to Francesca over the phone on Friday, and before Francesca could even reply she'd added, 'Oh, I know what everyone *says*, but I don't believe it. About the drugs, and all.

'I took Kayla, my four-year-old, to him a month ago when she had a fever of 104 on a Saturday afternoon and Dr Stock just had his machine on, telling people to go to the emergency room at Wayans Falls. Anyway, he was fabulous. I've seen that druggy look, and he doesn't have it. He answered all my questions in detail, and took a throat culture—and it *was* strep—and Kayla loved him.

'I told my sister to go to him for her pregnancy, and she is, and she thinks he's great, too. So I'm sorry, Dr Brady, nothing personal, but I'm no longer looking for a job.'

…Which meant she'd had to draft a classified advertisement for the *Wayans Falls Sentinel* today to advertise the position.

Mrs Mayberry was sceptical about this bringing any reliable responses. 'I always think word of mouth is best,' she had said this morning, after bringing in coffee at nine then stopping halfway into the office with her mouth dropped open in consternation as she remembered this was against her orders. Immediately, she was near to tears.

Francesca had had to soothe her and tell her it didn't

matter, and that actually she *did* feel like a cup this morning after all—which was a concession she'd probably live to regret. Poor Mrs Mayberry was painfully eager to please these days…

She put the stethoscope to Eric Saltman's chest and listened front and back in several places while he breathed in and out. He did seem to have a touch of flu. There was some upper respiratory congestion. Nothing, though, that was suggestive of anything worse than this, such as pneumonia. And yet he was burning up. She could feel the heat he was throwing off, even without touching him, and when she listened to his heart it was galloping.

She stepped back. 'Well, Mr Saltman…'

She glanced at his chart again and registered the fact that he had lost another four pounds in the past week. Hyperthyroidism. The diagnosis screamed at her, and yet the test had shown—

'No! Make it go back! Make it go back!'

'I beg your pardon?' She whipped around. Mr Saltman had been looking past her, his ill face betraying terror and those classic, protruding eyes even more staring than usual. But there was nothing frightening there. Nothing that *she* could see, anyway.

'What is it, Mr Saltman?' she begged, thoroughly unnerved now.

'The door… It's lunging at me. Make it go back. It's going to press me against the wall!'

He was retreating now, whimpering, and she called quickly, her own voice betraying alarm, 'Dixie? Dixie, I need you in the blue room right now, please!'

Dixie appeared, wide-eyed and breathless, unused to such an urgent summons, and Francesca pushed her back through the open door and whispered desperately, 'Mr Saltman is hallucinating. Try and keep him calm for half a minute while I…'

While she what? There was only one obvious answer,

but she didn't want to even consider it. Seconds later, she knew she had to.

'While I call Dr Wilde.'

'OK, but what shall I do if he…?'

'You handle it, Dixie,' she begged. 'You're very capable.'

In her office she seized the phone and prayed he'd be there, not out on some carpenter's mission to the hardware store. He had finished varnishing the porch and was starting to renovate the upper trim now.

'Hello.' The rather dark, dusky baritone voice came after just two rings and she almost cried into the phone with relief.

'Luke.'

'Chess… Is it?'

'Yes! Thank God you're there! I've got Eric Saltman here. My nurse, Dixie, is with him right now. He's delusional. His serum T4 came back normal. Now he's sick with something. Fever's 104, he says. Feels even hotter to me. And his whole presentation is so *classic* for thyroid. I don't know if it's all connected but it seems like it must be, only I'm not *seeing* it and I should be! It's been such a crazy week, though—'

'I'll be right up,' was all he said, and then he'd put down the phone.

She was shaking and wondering why on earth she'd ever thought she wanted to be in family practice where, as it suddenly seemed to her, you had to be able to diagnose a million different ailments from variants of the same three symptoms. But she couldn't just hide in here like a complete coward, waiting for Luke. Dixie was probably panicking.

'As if I'm *not*!' she muttered aloud.

She hurried into the blue room again. Eric Saltman's breathing was rapid and shallow, and his blood-shot eyes were glazed. His skin was dry and obviously burning, and he was still staring in a terrified way at the door, the window and the room's storage closet, as if each of them were advancing on him like some crazed yet cunning monster.

'Mr Saltman…'

'Stop it! Stop it!'

'We *are* stopping it, Mr Saltman. Dr Wilde is coming to stop it now.'

As if on cue, they heard striding footsteps outside and Luke came through the door, already speaking.

'If in doubt,' he said to Francesca, 'first trust your clinical judgement and, second, order more tests. It's OK, Mr Saltman,' he soothed the patient, interrupting himself. 'We're going to deal with this, all right?' Then he turned to Francesca again. 'You tested for serum T4 last week, right?'

'Yes, and it came back—'

'Normal.' He nodded. 'Let's put up an IV.'

He looked at Dixie, and she disappeared at once to bring what was needed. She was efficient and would soon be back, Francesca knew.

'But did you test for T3?'

She shook her head. 'There seemed no point in adding to the expense of the tests.'

'Because there is the odd occasion when the serum T4 level can be quite normal— Thanks, uh, Dixie. Now, drugs. We need…' He rattled off a list. Francesca recognised them all, and had them all on hand.

He set up the intravenous line with amazing swiftness, drew up the drugs and began to infuse them, along with fluid at a rapid rate of flow. There was a beta-blocker to slow his heart and metabolism, a couple of different drugs to start controlling the thyroid output and something to reduce the fever. Only once the clear fluid was dripping into the tubing did he turn back to Francesca to finish his earlier sentence.

'While the serum T3 level is raised, confirming the clinical picture—in this case quite apparent, as you've said—of hyperthyroidism. And this looks like a case of flu precipitating a thyroid storm on top of the original illness, which I suspect will turn out to be Graves's disease. Mr Saltman, you'll start to feel a little better soon, but you *will* need a day or two in hospital. We'll call an ambulance.' Again he turned to Dixie, and she nodded and went to do it at once.

'No,' the ill man managed. 'My wife… If the door starts coming at her…'

'No one else at home?'

'No. She's on a…a…' he made a tremendous effort '…a home monitor for her pre-term labour, but—'

'We'll send the ambulance up for her, too, then. Dr Brady?'

Francesca nodded. 'That seems best.'

'OK, then. Good.' He nodded, then drawled darkly, 'Mind if I head back now? You never know, I may actually have a patient of my own. I'm officially open for another ten minutes, and my new secretary doesn't start until next week.'

'Luke…' She followed him out the door.

'Yes?' he turned reluctantly.

'I—' What did you say to someone who clearly wanted to be gone?

'Don't be upset that you missed it,' he pre-empted her coolly.

But she shook her head, mute. She *was* upset, and now his face and tone softened.

'Look, it's the kind of thing you know like the back of your hand three days before the exam, but in your first month of real, qualified practice it flies right out the window. You'll soon relax and get all your facts and your judgement back where they belong.'

If you'd take a few of my *patients* it might help, she threatened darkly and silently, adding aloud, 'But, Luke, I thought you'd only recently started practising here yourself. Two months?'

'About that,' he nodded. 'But I was in a group practice in Saratoga for a year and a half before I ditched it to come back here. Crazy, wasn't I?' he commented cynically.

'Things are starting to pick up for you now, though,' she hazarded. 'You've got Lyn Parker starting.'

'Yes, things are picking up,' he agreed equably. 'I had four whole patients today, and two of them will need to come back. Employing Mrs Parker is an act of defiance, Chess. I'm fond of those. Don't you remember? Like riding a Harley at eighteen? Like coming back here! Let's just hope I can still eat at the end of the month after I've paid her!'

'It *will* pick up for you, Luke,' she insisted, though totally at a loss as to why she kept breaking her ego against his like this. The professional co-operation she envisaged was never going to happen. Was she too stubborn? Or did she just have no pride?

'It's your faith in me that keeps me going, princess,' he drawled sarcastically.

It was a parting line that left her hot with fury and, although it was somehow cold comfort, more pride than you could shake a stick at.

'He's resting comfortably now,' Dixie reported when Francesca returned to the blue room. 'Temp still sky-high. 104.7.'

'The medication will bring it down soon. And we have a cooling blanket, don't we?'

'Yes,' Dixie nodded. 'I was going to ask you if—'

'Definitely. You know where it is?'

'I certainly do!' Then she added with a grin, 'Hey, and it was *real* interesting to see Dr Wilde up close and personal. I hadn't realised he was such a hunk!'

The ambulance had arrived within half an hour, and would detour to the Saltmans' house in the woods to pick up Gina Saltman, before heading back to Wayans Falls. Francesca put in a call to endocrinologist Steve Kagan, whom Luke had recommended, because the obvious thing to do now was to perform a radioactive iodine uptake test to establish the diagnosis for certain and to determine the best form of therapy.

She didn't detail to Dr Kagan her initial confusion over the anomalous test result. He didn't need to hear it. She still felt bad about it, though, and reluctantly grateful to Luke for being available, willing and on top of what to do.

She'd never thanked him, she realised, and she really should.

Out of professional courtesy, if nothing else. The knowledge that he wouldn't appreciate her thanks and would, in fact, be angered by it more than anything else made her perversely more determined. By hook or by crook, she would *not* be the one to behave badly!

Dixie and Mrs Mayberry had both gone now so she could do it at once. Or she could wait until tomorrow, but by then she'd probably have stopped seething over that unforgivable word 'princess' and since she definitely wanted to confront him on that...

'Don't you *ever* call me "princess" again in any context!' she told him without preamble ten minutes later, marching through his waiting room and pushing open his office door, which was slightly ajar.

He looked up from a desk covered in textbooks and medical journals, and gave an evil grin.

'You've come to thank me, obviously, for helping you today.'

'Yes, I have, actually,' she agreed darkly, 'but first I have this other little matter to get out of the way. Just *don't*, OK? I'm *not* a princess. I might have been one once—'

'Might?'

'OK, I *was*. But I'm not now. I practically *fired* Mrs

Mayberry last week. That wasn't princess—that was wicked witch, in anyone's book.'

'Fired Mrs Mayberry? OK,' he drawled, 'you've proved your point.'

He sat back. He was still wearing his doctor disguise, though she hadn't even registered the fact earlier during the emergency over Eric Saltman. Dark pants, a white shirt, a neutral, patterned tie. Evidently he wasn't working on the house today. What *was* he doing?

She glanced down at the litter of learned matter on his desk, and he followed the direction of her grey gaze.

'Circumcision,' he said. 'I've got a pregnant patient who knows she's having twin boys and wants my opinion on it. I don't want to let her down. Her husband and I used to fix bikes together so I'm trying to arrive at a definitive conclusion on the issue.'

'Well, you won't do it by reading books,' Francesca said honestly.

'I'm beginning to realise that. Although I think if I stacked them, pro circumcision on my right and con on my left, pro would come out somewhat higher these days.'

'While con would make a very vocal minority.'

'And where do you stand?'

'On your right. Pro,' she answered at once.

'Because?'

'Because my favourite professor at medical school was pro,' she confessed, making a face. 'That isn't a good reason, is it?'

'Depends,' he conceded, 'on who your favourite professor was.'

'Well, yes. He probably authored several of the books and articles you're reading.'

'This study suggesting that an intact foreskin increases the chances of HIV transmission three- or four-fold is pretty interesting,' Luke said, 'but no parent would want to think of their child being at risk for HIV some time in the future, I guess.'

'Perhaps the thing to consider is if you tell her *not* to have them circumcised are you going to feel comfortable explaining to her how to keep the foreskin area clean, and how to retract it safely later on?'

He looked at her for a moment, then said drily, 'Good point. So you're saying, Chess, that if I... How can I put this? That I shouldn't talk the talk if I can't walk the walk?'

'Yes,' she said, 'although I might not have put it in exactly those terms.'

'I think you've convinced me.'

He stood decisively as he spoke and began packing up the books and journals to return them to the neat but cheap bookshelves that lined one wall. This was a room that could be gorgeous, with its high ceilings, hardwood floors and wide bay window, but it wasn't well furnished enough to be gorgeous now, and the contrast between it and her own professionally decorated office was huge.

Instinctively, she began to help him re-shelve the books, her interest caught by several of the titles. His small, private research library was more than adequate and up to date.

The task of shelving the books brought her close to him and made her aware of him in a way she hadn't had time to be an hour ago as they'd worked together over Eric Saltman. Suddenly it was disturbing in its strength and familiarity.

Ready to leave, she packed the last of the books just as he reached up past her to put in a set of journals, and his shirtsleeve brushed her forearm. The fine hairs there stood on end at once, and she felt the warm fan of his breath against her hair. She said quickly, 'Look, I've gotten distracted. I really came to... I do sincerely want to thank you for—'

'No, you don't,' he muttered, his tone a threat to expose them both totally. 'You want to kiss me. Just like I want to kiss you. I've been kicking myself that I didn't do it last week when I had the chance.'

He pulled her hungrily against him and she went at once without resistance. There was no room in her mind at all to think of anything but her surging physical response to him, and the confidence of his actions made this very, very easy for her.

He wrapped his arms around her and swooped down to find her mouth, parting her lips and exploring them with the utter certainty that she would respond. And she did, stretching her face upwards, closing her eyes and pressing against him.

'Oh, Chess,' he groaned. 'What do you do to me? I really thought I'd hate you!' His hands slid up her back to caress her nape then lift her hair. 'I couldn't believe I still wanted to do this to you!'

'Luke…' Her strength was going, and all she wanted to do was to loll against him, feel the male hardness of his arms and chest, taste him and graze her face against the prickly new growth of beard that was already perceptible after his morning shave.

'It's the same for you, isn't it?' he demanded, cupping her jaw between his hands and boring into her with his hot blue gaze. 'You don't believe it either, but you feel it.'

'Yes. Oh, yes!' The words were lost against his lips and she closed her eyes again, feeling that this was heaven—something she had wanted all her life, without even knowing it existed. Her hands pressed against his chest then climbed to his neck, which was smooth and warm and tanned, and then… She couldn't resist any longer. She *had* to see how it would feel now that his walnut brown hair was longer, falling on his head in thick, soft waves… She reached up and *mussed* it, tangling her fingers there, caressing the well-shaped curve of his head, thoroughly ruining the rather neat, conservative style that he'd adopted to go with his doctor clothes. His doctor clothes.

'It's no good your dressing like that, Luke,' she told him hazily, bringing her hands down again to caress the soft cotton of his shirt and pluck at his tie. 'You might fool some people, but you don't fool me. I know what's underneath this. It's the same body you had at eighteen, strong and hard and beautiful.'

'And you want it, don't you?' he muttered darkly into her hair. 'Just like I want yours—the softness of you, the resilience, your princess hair— No, let me say it! Let me!' He pressed his fingers across her mouth to stifle her protest and pulled away enough to look at her, his blue eyes blazing. 'It's not an insult. You always seemed so totally unattainable, and now to find that you're *stirred* by this just as I am. It's… It's… Chess, I'm on fire!'

She made a little sound in her throat, too overwhelmed to speak, and he held her again, trembling with male need. The sheer force of it frightened her enough to bring her a measure of control at last, and she turned her head away and laid it to his chest, listening to the hammering of his heartbeat.

'I hope you don't get any late patients, Luke,' she managed, 'because I don't think I closed the outer door.'

'Would it be a problem if we were caught?' he growled. 'We're consenting adults, and we're fully clothed. Although the idea of our *not* being…'

'Well, I've never found the possibility of discovery to be at all erotic,' she said.

'Not erotic,' he agreed. 'Not shameful, though.'

'But it's not that,' she persisted. 'There's a lot more going on here than just a kiss.'

'I know,' he growled. 'There's my heart practically bursting in my chest, and my guts on fire and my head swimming with images of you…'

'No, Luke!'

'No,' he suddenly conceded, pulling away. They weren't touching any more, and she still wanted to so badly she throbbed with it. 'No, you're right,' he went on. 'We don't need to spell it out, do we? This is rocking the boat badly. This was *not* part of the programme!'

He was silent, thinking. He had turned away from her, and she watched his back, the muscles there rippling beneath his shirt as he lifted his arms to lace his fingers behind his head.

She waited another moment, then said, not wanting to, 'I'll go, Luke.'

'Don't!' He wheeled around. 'I'm not saying... Just don't, OK? Let's...eat or something.'

He looked at his watch and narrowed his eyes, as if calculating something.

'I'd like that,' she answered.

'Let's get out of town.' It was decisive. 'There's a good Chinese restaurant halfway between Wayans Falls and Stedman Point. A bit over half an hour. Too far?'

'No, not too far.'

'Good, because I'd like a drive. Do you need to go home?' His gaze flicked briefly over her patterned sapphire-blue button-through skirt and matching silk blouse. 'From my point of view, you're just fine.'

'I— Thanks.' How ludicrous it was to be bowled over by a casual compliment like that. Was it his voice, still heavy with desire, as hers was husky with it? She gathered herself. 'No, I don't need to go home. The place is all locked and I have my pager and phone.'

'Wait here. Give me a minute. Then let's go.'

He disappeared into the private part of the house, shut the door behind him and she heard a few nondescript sounds—the creak of the fridge door opening, his footsteps, water running. A few minutes later he was back, striding to reach into his desk drawer and pull out a bunch of keys. Five minutes later they were in his car, which was adequate if not luxurious.

He took the back roads, not the highway, rattling over

the big wooden bridge across the Buckhorn River on the east side of town, then up over a ridge of mountain and down to Lake Edward. The road skirted the big lake, dipping and curving past signs for the expensive and exclusive resorts and motels that spread along the lake's foreshores.

The light was just starting to fade and there were clouds building in the west to create a glorious pile of sunset shapes and colours. The lake was glass-smooth today, glimpsed through the pines, and shining with light. There were a couple of boats out late, and barely broken reflections of the blue mountain shapes.

'I love this landscape,' Luke said. It was the first time he had spoken during the drive.

'I know,' Francesca answered. 'I'd get hungry for it during my years of college and training in New York, but somehow Mom and Dad always came down. They were always rather over-protective of my study schedule. Guess they were terrified I'd fail!'

'Not likely.'

'And then for vacations we went to Florida. Europe twice, too. When I came back a week and a half ago it was only my third trip here in twelve years. That seems crazy now. How about you, Luke?'

'Yeah, I've been back,' he growled. 'Like you, not often. I lived in New Jersey for a while, and I went to medical school in Ohio.'

'Oh, I hadn't realised.'

They talked about those years for the rest of the drive and into the meal, sharing horror stories of internship, discovering shared milestones in their evolution as doctors. Their first sense of real competence as doctors, their first experience with a life-threatening illness. They took their time, sharing plates of delicate hors d'oeuvres followed by two spicy dishes served with fluffy white rice. Cool, dry white wine slipped down effortlessly as well, and added its own ingredient of relaxation to the already potent mix between them.

He didn't bother to disguise his desire for her. It smouldered in him blatantly across the table, reflected in his blue eyes and in his crooked, caressing smile. He didn't refer again to what was happening between them, didn't acknowledge it with a kiss or a touch, but they both recognised it quite starkly all the same.

There was something dangerous about it. About *him*. Because she knew somehow that their desire didn't fully cancel out their wariness, their questions about each other, their anger. Their two responses to each other existed independently, and while at this moment it was desire that had crowded to the fore she knew that the anger, in particular, was still there, awaiting its turn.

Shockingly, the idea didn't turn her off. On the contrary, she knew that the thought of dealing with him as an adversary was licking at the corners of her awareness, like flame licking at the edge of paper, heating her blood still more, and suddenly she understood that it had always been that way. She had always wanted the wildest part of him. She hadn't really wanted to tame him fifteen years ago— she'd wanted to be part of what he was.

Now, with all those extra years under her belt, and the confidence and experience she'd acquired along with a degree in medicine, she had grown into a worthwhile opponent, someone who could be that vital bit dangerous herself, should the occasion require it. Tonight she wondered just how far she would dare to go.

After the meal, when they reached his car, he seemed restless and leaned across the top of it to say, 'Let's not go home just yet. It's a nice night. Let's drive down to the lake.' He glanced at the thin silk of her blouse and added, 'I'll keep you warm.'

How could four casual words make her insides roil like that?

The tourist season in Stedman Point was not yet in full swing so he parked easily down by the mini-golf course and they walked along the walled lake-front, down past where the paddle-steamers docked between their short cruises. Silver-blue light shimmered on the black water, and there were some insomniac ducks bobbing around, hoping to be fed.

'Sorry, guys,' Luke told them. 'We have other things to do.'

Like continuing their discovery of one another. He lifted her onto the low wall, which made her seem taller than him and forced him to stretch and her to bend. And that was new and wonderful—to feel his mouth travelling down her neck so that he could nuzzle with tantalising heat at the swelling slopes of her breasts, to feel his hands gripping her hips as he bent to lift her blouse and deliberately tickle her navel with his tongue.

Next, he leaped up onto the wall beside her and it felt more familiar—to have him taller so that she could arch to reach him or pillow her head on his chest and hear his heart.

The wind blew across the water, tangling her blonde hair and whipping that stray brown lock down onto his forehead, but he did as he had promised and held her so she wasn't cold.

They didn't speak much, just kissed crazily, tasted each other, melted against each other, until it got dangerous for both of them and he managed huskily, 'Home?'

'Yes.'

This time he didn't waste precious minutes on the scenic route, but took the side streets through Stedman Point and hit the highway as soon as he could, burning up it in the darkness until the turn-off for Darrensberg…Route Nineteen…State Street…home.

Her place. He stopped out the front and she heard herself

saying with a catch in her throat and a casual intonation that fooled neither of them, 'Coffee?'

'Sure. We need to talk, actually—amongst other things.'

She knew it was a mistake the moment they got inside.

CHAPTER SIX

LUKE had seen her professional rooms the other day but he hadn't seen the private part of the house, and it wasn't until Francesca had shut the front door and begun to lead him along the Persian carpet runner that covered the polished hardwood of the wide hall that she saw it all through his eyes and realised how much the luxury of the house's furnishings shouted her father's professional success.

Worse, how much it shouted the fact that their connection to each other, while defying all logic with its physical strength, was still riddled through and through with unresolved issues—distrust, hostility and an embarrassing disparity in professional circumstances being only three of them.

They went past a piece of antique pottery on a special stand, and an original nineteenth-century oil painting of Lake Edward and its surrounding peaks. In the kitchen the new and startlingly white twin fridge-freezer unit hummed quietly, and the glass fronts of the expensively remodelled cabinets shone.

The electric coffee machine had already been programmed by Mrs Mayberry to make Francesca's breakfast cup at seven forty-five so she had to change the setting, which was impossible to do casually as she had to think for a moment about exactly how to get it off the pre-programmed timer and have it start to make coffee right now.

'I don't know why people have these things,' she muttered. 'More trouble than they're worth.'

'Evidently,' was all he said.

He was standing in the middle of the room, shoulders

hunched and hands thrust down into the pockets of his
smart doctor pants, and he only looked out of place because
he clearly felt that way. Francesca, meanwhile, felt just like
the 'princess' he had derided her as, and she hated it.

This was all Mom and Dad. This wasn't her. The almost
eerily silent dishwasher, the shining stainless-steel sinks,
the valuable majolica fruit bowl. She didn't think twice
about this kitchen. It wasn't important to her—and that was
half the problem, she suddenly realised. Luke couldn't afford the luxury of disdaining all this.

Fumbling with the plastic coffee scoop, she spilled a
scattering of the rich granules onto the granite counter top,
and turned away in disgust at herself.

'I hate this. I'm sorry. Do you really want coffee?' Then
she added quickly, 'Oh, of course you do! You said...' She
looked around vaguely for something to wipe up the spill,
but he was at her side before she could even move.

'Chess...'

He turned her into his arms and held her, his mouth mov-
ing over hers, parting her lips, tasting her, drinking her as
she whimpered a little with the delight and suddenness of
it. He thrust his hands up beneath the silk of her blouse to
cup her instantly swollen breasts and she shuddered and
strained against him, wanting more.

'You're quite full,' he muttered, caressing her nipples
into tight, tingling peaks. 'You overflow my hands with
your softness. You feel...amazing.'

She couldn't speak, could only stand there with eyes
closed, frozen by the ecstasy of what he was doing to her.
He had begun to slip undone the buttons of her blouse, and
a moment later he had peeled it from her shoulders, flicked
aside the satin straps of her bra and unhooked the catch so
that her breasts spilled fully from the lacy cups and into
his hands.

He groaned as she arched and wantonly offered him the
full globes he seemed to take such pleasure in, and his

pleasure became so tangled with hers that they were indistinguishable.

She plucked at his shirt, wanting to feel his skin, but there was no time to tackle his buttons properly so she gave up and just focused on his kiss, his touch.

'I want to take you upstairs,' he whispered. 'I want to make love to you, Chess.'

'I know. That's… That's… I want it, too.'

'But this isn't what I planned.'

'Do plans matter?'

'We were going to talk. We *have* to talk before we go any further with this.'

His fingers slid along her ribs, as if trying to hang onto her until the last possible second, then he pulled away and stood facing her, frowning darkly, while she simply watched him, frozen and wide-eyed, still breathless with sensation, her hands pressed behind her against the countertop.

'I need to know,' he went on through clenched teeth, 'just what your father has said to you. Just how far you two are accomplices.'

'My father? What does he have to do with this?' It seemed incongruous that they were standing here wanting each other—her bare, swollen breasts still pulsed and tingled—and he was asking some obscure question about her *father*. 'Accomplices?' she echoed blankly.

'God, I haven't got the strength to beat around the bush, Francesca,' he growled. 'Do you think it's an accident of fate that your place looks like this and your practice is bursting at the seams, while my house is as shabby as a well-used couch and I'm lucky to see a dozen patients a week?'

'No, of course not. I've heard the stories. Those things are hard to live down, Luke. Especially if—'

Luke cut in. 'Especially if a rival is doing his damnedest

to make sure the stories—the rumours—are fanned, inflated, corroborated.'

'A rival? Are you saying it was *my father* who spread the stories?'

'Started them, not spread them,' he corrected. 'Dr Brady didn't need to do any spreading. Other people did that for him. A hint here and a hint there. That was enough for him. He probably said it all very reluctantly—bad-mouthing a colleague, after all. No one wants to betray the profession. That's the impression he would have given, and it carried all the more weight that way.

'To suggest avidly, at every possible opportunity, that the other doctor in town drank, and supplied drugs to his son, and covered up a sordid affair with flagrant medical malpractice—that might have made people suspicious of his motives, but to suggest it *reluctantly* and only to one or two carefully chosen people—'

'This is outrageous!'

Angrily, she reached for the colourful heap on the floor that was her blouse, slung it across her shoulders and thrust her arms through the sleeves, not bothering with the buttons or with her bra, which was similarly heaped on the floor. She regretted the latter omission a moment later, though, because even now, in the midst of her anger, her nipples were still treacherously hard against the cold silk.

Impatiently, with shaking fingers, she knotted the two front panels of fabric tightly beneath her breasts and said hotly, 'This is totally outrageous! What's wrong with you, Luke, that you have to scapegoat my father this way for *your* father's…well, let's just say his failings as a doctor, and for your own—'

She stopped. The issue of his drug use. She'd grabbed at it because, in her hurt and anger, she was looking for a weapon and it was the nearest weapon to hand, but when it came to the point she knew it was a weapon she wasn't prepared to use. Not yet. Not till she knew more. She still felt compelled to give him the benefit of the doubt.

'My own what, Chess?' he demanded dangerously.

'Past,' she filled in weakly.

'My past,' he echoed derisively. 'God, don't you think I'm strong enough, *good* enough, to overcome that in people's minds if that was all it was? I wasn't *that* wild, you know, although it was a convenient label. Wilde by name, and so on. If it was just a question of my past I'd have the town eating out of my hand by now, but when I'm fighting against something deliberate, something that's designed to drive me out as it was designed to drive my father out...

'And it's still going on! There's someone in this town still spreading the stuff. I've had Lyn Parker say to me she "doesn't believe what everyone says" about my drug use. So who's saying it?'

His eyes blazed and he towered over her threateningly.

But she was too angry to be cowed by his physical presence.

'Me. You're accusing me, aren't you?'

'No! But I do wonder if you know.'

She wasn't listening. 'Merely accusing my father isn't enough. God, and to think I've been so scrupulously trying to be fair, to avoid a rush to judgement. Amazingly enough, I'm still trying to!' She gave a bitter laugh, then met his blazing blue gaze.

He was trying to judge *her* now. She could see it. Weighing her words to see if they contained the full truth. After several long moments of silence he said slowly, 'Trying to be fair? I guess there's some virtue in that. You've accused me of scapegoating. I've accused your father of deliberate rumour-mongering, and you of knowing at least something about that. I think we've both got enough to chew on for the rest of the night so I'll retire to consider the question, if you don't mind.'

'I don't mind at all!' she lied at once. She felt riven in

two. She *didn't* believe his accusations, she certainly didn't want to—and yet she still wanted him.

He was already out of the kitchen, though, and striding silently along that beautiful stretch of Persian carpet.

'Luke!' She ran after him, hating the frail sound of her voice in the air. 'Luke! Surely we should at least try to—'

Her voice was far firmer this time, but he didn't stop, just drawled tiredly over his shoulder, 'Sleep on it, Francesca.'

But as he left the house, slamming the door behind him, she felt further from sleep than she had ever been in her life.

Slowly, she walked back to the kitchen, reset the coffee-machine, wiped up the spilled grounds and put the coffee-can away, then picked up her bra and crumpled it in one hand, before switching off the light with the other. The house was quite silent, but then, as she came through the hall, the antique grandfather clock in her father's library at the front of her house began to chime and she counted the strokes disbelievingly.

Ten, eleven, twelve... It was midnight, and this Cinderella of an evening had sure turned into a pumpkin!

To make those accusations about Dad! He's so bitter, and he's brooded on it all for so long. *His* dad's dead, and perhaps that makes it too hard for him to admit that old Dr Wilde wasn't a success. Perhaps it challenges Luke's own manhood as well to believe that.

Plausible, nice psychobabble, but none of it rang true. She recognised beyond anything how much strength there was in Luke—too much for him to need the emotional prop of believing himself persecuted.

'The whole thing is just impossible!' she said aloud.

She climbed the stairs and felt her breasts bouncing inside their inadequate covering of silk. In the bathroom, ready to set about her habitual nightly tooth-brushing, she was dismayed at the picture she presented in the mirror.

Her hair was wildly tousled, and that knot in her blouse bared her midriff and pushed her breasts up so that they displayed an invitingly full cleavage.

Despite the incongruity of her pager clipped to her belt, she looked quite wanton, messy with passion. And it's how I still feel, too, she thought, appalled. I'm appalled and furious and I still want him.

The evidence was there in the tight beading of her nipples against the silk, as she remembered his hands cupping and caressing her, and in the way her breathing immediately quickened as she thought of how close she had come to having him up here.

She doubted they'd have made it as far as the bed. There was another wonderfully soft carpet in this upstairs hall. To have fallen there with him and slid those incongruously neat clothes from his masculine frame so that she could feel him pressed against her, length to length…

Shuddering, she fled the bathroom and found the sanctuary of her bedroom, stripping hastily to reach for her very demure cotton and lace nightgown. She had only just let it fall around her when she heard a car turning from the back lane into the space in front of the garage, and then a minute later a loud knock came at the door. He had come back to finish this face to face!

That was the only thought that filled her mind as she hurried downstairs again, and she didn't stop to think that this didn't fit the facts at all until she had pulled open the front door, her face filled with an absurd mingling of eagerness, anger and desire.

To find her parents standing there, her father leaning tiredly on his wife's arm.

She stopped short. 'Mom! Dad! What on earth—?'

'Well, if you didn't think it was us, honey, you shouldn't have opened the door like that,' her father pointed out, with perfect truth, in his still frighteningly frail voice. 'It's after midnight.'

'I know. I wasn't thinking.' She had to think now, and quickly—had to push all that awareness of Luke aside and focus on her parents instead. She said with more control, 'But it *is* you so...'

She stood back and they entered, each bringing a small suitcase and sensibly dressed in pale, comfortable travel clothes.

'We would have been here an hour ago, too,' Frank Brady said, 'if your mother hadn't insisted on stopping for a proper restaurant meal.'

'You were exhausted, dear,' Jean Brady soothed, then she added to Francesca, 'He just can't accept the change of pace!'

'You didn't tell me you were coming up,' Francesca said, following them down the hall. She tried not to make it sound like an accusation.

'Well, we did want to surprise you, in any case...' her mother explained. She was heading towards the kitchen. 'By coming to see how you were getting along. We would have waited longer, but when we heard—'

'That you'd been so needlessly cruel to poor Betty,' her father came in heatedly, switching on the kitchen light and going to the fridge, his gait clumsy. He had aged, Francesca saw, even in the three months since she had last seen him. He got out the milk and turned to her with a pained look on his face.

'Francesca, how *could* you! She was in tears to me on the phone, and even more upset when she discovered that you hadn't even thought it worthwhile to tell me about it yourself. She's been with the practice for twenty-five years, and you upset her so much in a week that she was forced to resign. She's convinced you did it deliberately, you realise.'

'I was going to tell you, of course. I wanted your advice on a present, or a bonus.'

'Under the circumstances, both!' her father said.

He was flushed and breathing heavily. Francesca pulled a kitchen chair up behind him and almost forced him to sit down, saying, 'But I was waiting until I'd found a replacement because I thought you'd worry if—'

'Unless we can get her to change her mind,' Mrs Brady interposed, pouring milk into two mugs and putting them in the microwave to heat. 'It ought to be possible. If your father goes to her and—'

'It'll take some smoothing over, that's for certain,' he cut in. 'It's not exactly how I imagined...' He wheezed, then continued, 'Spending my first visit to my daughter in her new practice, but it can be managed. I know Betty. She'll do it for my sake.'

'But, Dad, I don't *want* her back,' Francesca said desperately. 'And I'm horrified that she called you to complain about the whole thing. *She* was the one to suggest resigning, said she was too set in her ways to make the change, and I didn't argue because it was true. She couldn't even remember to bring me coffee at the time I asked for it.'

'You mean this is all over a little thing like coffee?' Frank Brady wheezed again.

'Speaking of which,' his wife came in, 'where's the hot chocolate mix, honey?'

'I don't have any.'

'But I left two full packets in February.'

'Preston must have drunk it, then. And I don't like hot chocolate so I didn't buy any myself.'

'So I've heated this milk for nothing? Well, that's a nuisance.'

'Does it really matter?' Francesca asked desperately, feeling swamped. 'It's after midnight. Dad, you need to rest, and I was about to go to bed myself. I've got a full day of appointments tomorrow, and if I happen to get called out as well—'

'Oh well, as to that, I can take over for a couple of hours tomorrow afternoon if you want to go shopping with your mother or take a nap,' Frank Brady offered at once. 'I'm not completely out to pasture quite yet! And I'm sure people would like to see me back for a guest spot, so to speak, as much as I'd enjoy it myself.'

'Dad, no! You're exhausted! And this is *my* practice now,' she begged.

'And, anyway, Frank, you'll be resting all morning, then taking poor Betty to lunch, I shouldn't wonder,' her mother suggested.

'Take her to lunch, by all means,' Francesca agreed, 'but *don't* try to persuade her to stay, Dad! She's just too used to you. Too loyal. Obviously she must appreciate what a marvellous doctor you were—are—'

'I hadn't realised it was possible to be too loyal,' Frank Brady grumbled.

'Well, it is, and I'm sorry if she's upset about what happened, but she should have come to me about it, not gone running to you with the waterworks switched on.'

Her parents looked shocked at her impatient tone, and she apologised quickly. 'Look, it's been a long eight days. I'm sorry. The practice is swamped with patients, and I'm…really tired. Can we all go to bed and see how things look in the morning?'

'That's a sensible plan,' Jean Brady agreed, turning in appeal to her husband.

With gruff reluctance, he nodded. 'Put the mugs of milk back in the fridge, then. I'll have milk coffee in the morning.'

The Gables restaurant was almost empty the next evening, and the Brady family were treated as honoured guests, with lavish concern for old Dr Brady's health and complimentary plates of hors d'oeuvres in addition to what they had ordered from the lavish menu.

They were ushered deferentially to the best table, in front of the big bay window that overlooked Buckhorn Park, and

Francesca felt rather self-conscious as the group of tourists two tables distant eyed them curiously, as if hoping to spot a celebrity. They'd be disappointed. Frank Brady's status was purely a local phenomenon.

That status did exist, though. The Gables had been here for fifteen years now, and Dr Brady had delivered each of the proprietor's children, as well as treating him for a severe scald several years ago after a kitchen mishap. There were a lot of people in Darrensberg who had similar reasons for gratitude towards Frank Brady.

Surely there were people who must feel that way about James Wilde, too! Francesca had been desperate to ask her father about it all day. She'd slept badly again last night, despite the fact that there had been no call-outs or phone consults. At least her parents' arrival had thoroughly dampened down her body's stubborn and overwhelming desire for Luke.

What he had said to her refused to go away, though—the cruel and very deliberate accusations he had made. She hadn't been able to get them out of her mind, even during the day's parade of patients, and it was fortunate, perhaps, that all the complaints had been routine.

Now, as she spooned up spicy carrot and coriander soup from her plate, she had her first real opportunity to broach the subject, and she found that her palms were growing damp at the thought. She *didn't* want to hear awful stories about Luke's past—and his present—convincingly confirmed by her parents. So what *did* she want to hear? That Luke was right to have accused her father?

'I was stunned to find Luke Wilde in practice here when I arrived,' she said conversationally, putting down her spoon and watching her father's face while trying to seem very casual.

'He's crazy to do it!' Frank Brady answered. 'I couldn't believe it when Betty told me the other night. I'd thought the Wilde practice was dead and buried. But don't worry,' he finished, his gesture containing a frail authority, 'he can't last.'

'Oh, I'm not worried,' she answered quickly. 'That is, I hope he *does* last. There's plenty of room for two doctors here.'

'Yes, but that's your opportunity to offer a partnership,' her father grumbled impatiently. 'Build up your own practice, Chessie, that's the way to go. Ask around. Hunt up some old friends from medical school who have good track records and let one of them buy in. Times are getting tough, even in medicine. *Especially* in medicine! That's why I worked so hard to leave you the practice in as good a position as I could. Twelve years ago, when you first started pre-med courses at college, I began to think of building your patient base.'

'Twelve years ago?' She was aghast. 'But I told you then that I was going into obstetrics. I had no intention of—'

'Oh, but I knew you'd come round. It's what I always intended—to leave the practice to one of my children.'

'But, Dad, I had to practically blackmail you into retiring three months ago!'

'Oh, yes,' he conceded wryly. 'I'd have put it off a little longer if I could, but you and your mother between you got your way in the end. I'm putty in your hands, you see.'

Francesca was the one who felt like putty! She had thought she'd won a huge battle in convincing her father to let her take over the practice, only to find now that it was what he'd wanted for her all along. He was certainly a man who liked to retain control, and who was convinced he knew best!

'A partnership was always out of the question for me,' he was saying now. 'I've always been too grumpy and arrogant to work well with anyone else.' He laughed comfortably. 'But I know a partnership would suit you. So think about it, why don't you, as soon as you're settled? Give me the pleasure of seeing you well set up, Chessie.'

The frailty was back suddenly, and she was tempted to see it as emotional manipulation, although she knew it was not.

'Perhaps Luke Wilde would like to buy in,' she suggested deliberately. She needed to test out all those absurd—if they *were* that absurd—accusations of last night.

And, as she'd half anticipated, her father exploded. 'That's a ludicrous suggestion!'

'Why, though? *Why*, Dad?'

'Because, if you're to stay in full control, you need someone who's not from here. You want to be undisputedly recognised as the senior partner, Francesca, so that *you* are the one people want to come to with the other guy—or another woman might work—a definite second choice. *You* want the pick of the patients, Chessie. I've told you, times are getting tough.'

He spread his hands expansively, but what his gesture took in didn't exactly support his argument—an expensive and elegant restaurant, with its deferential waiters and well-dressed diners. If the Brady family could afford to eat here on a regular basis—and they always had—then times couldn't be that tough, even with the complimentary dishes that Vincent Carillo threw in.

'With Luke as unpopular as he is, though,' Francesca pressed stubbornly, 'I'd scarcely have a problem keeping the pick of the patients if I took him in. Unless, of course, that unpopularity wasn't deserved, and people began to realise it.'

'Not deserved?' Frank said, his colour heightened and his breathing shallow. 'Of course it's deserved! He rode that terrible bike, he dropped out of school—'

'Fifteen years ago, Dad,' she pointed out quietly. 'And those things weren't crimes. He's changed, and old Dr Wilde is dead, yet he's dogged by terrible rumours that, as far as I've been able to discover, have no foundation in fact.'

'That's ridiculous!'

'Things like old Dr Wilde drinking and supplying Luke with drugs.'

'Yes, and everyone knew about it.'

'Everyone? Who's everyone? Who has concrete evidence? And who first spread the story? Did *you* have anything to do with it, Dad?'

'I knew about the stories, of course,' he answered. 'People said—'

'I know what people said. I've heard that at great length, but there hasn't been a shred of actual fact or detail, and there's plenty of evidence to the contrary. I'm asking you if you ever passed on the stories. Or if you started them.'

'That's a terrible accusation to make!'

'But is it true?'

'Luke had a girl pregnant. I saw them myself down in Wayans Falls one day. Then there was a girl who died giving birth up in some shack with James Wilde in attendance. Coincidence? Hardly! And the girl's own sister said—'

'Sharon Baron? Yes, I've met her. She's a reliable type!' Francesca had never used sarcasm like this to her father before and hated doing it, despite the hard expression she knew was carved on her face.

'Reliable or not, it seemed obvious that there had to be a connection.'

'Obvious,' Francesca repeated. 'So you started telling it as if it was fact?'

'Am I suddenly on trial here? I am!' He appealed to Francesca's mother.

'Of course you're not! Chessie, I don't know why you're—'

'Because Dad did it deliberately, didn't you Dad? You magnified every fragment of detail. You gave it your stamp of professional authority. You told it to me as if it was fact, too! I remember you told me he'd actually lost his licence to practice! You cast enough doubt on Dr Wilde that people stopped coming to him, and then it became a vicious cycle. His spirit broke, he couldn't keep the place up as it needed to be kept and that in itself became evidence of his incompetence, or his "drinking".'

'You don't understand, Francesca,' Frank Brady complained. 'All James Wilde was ever cut out for was family practice—general practice, as it was back then. I had the ability to be a specialist, and I'd have been one if things hadn't gone wrong at Harvard. Opportunities that should have gone to me went to someone else so I had to go in for rural medicine instead.

'But I *always* had a better mind than James Wilde. He came to me when he was in doubt about a diagnosis. Several times he admitted to me that he'd made mistakes. A missed pregnancy. A cancer he said was malignant, and it wasn't. It was better for the *town* that my practice should be the successful one. And better for you, too. Don't you think I owed it to everyone to make sure people were aware of even the shadow of a doubt over the state of the Wilde practice?'

'No,' she managed, her throat tight. 'No, I don't, Dad.'

'Well, you need to toughen up, then! You need to start seeing the world as it really is! There's no room for honour in it any more. I've known that since my college days, when Oliver Slade died and the residency he'd promised me went to a Princeton man instead.'

'That was wrong!' Jean Brady said, her cheeks pink with outrage. 'That shouldn't have happened! That residency should have been yours!'

'Dad, Luke Wilde is a good doctor, and yet he's failing here!'

'Well, then, he shouldn't have come back! The Brady practice is the one that this town needs!' He broke off. 'Ah, is that my lobster?' He turned with a frail smile to Vincent Carillo, who was serving them himself tonight. Frank

Brady's affable manner betrayed nothing of the family tension of a few moments ago. 'It looks stupendous, as usual!'

There seemed little left for Francesca to say, and her father clearly considered the subject closed.

Francesca's parents left again three days later. Their surprise visit had not been a success in anyone's terms. Mrs Mayberry was still leaving at the end of next week, only now she was completely convinced that Francesca actively disliked her and behaved like a mouse in the presence of an ogre, scuttling in and out and freezing in fear at the slightest suggestion of a cross word.

Francesca had never thought of herself as an ogre before, and to be cast in that role did not do a great deal for her good humour. Also, it was horrible to be so thoroughly confronted with the worst failings in each of her parents. Oh, she'd been dimly aware for some years that Dad had rather too high an opinion of himself, no tolerance for any perceived incompetence in others, little ability to put up with being crossed and a vague, lingering resentment over some piece of injustice from his training days.

She'd also known that Mom aided and abetted him in the continuance of these faults by her slavish agreement with almost everything he said. But to find that Dad's weakness—because she had to see all this as a weakness that went beyond his new physical frailty—had taken him as far as deliberately ruining a colleague's career. She felt sick about it and called her older sister, Louise, the night after her parents left to talk about it.

Louise had married and gone to live in Canada years ago, but at eight years Francesca's senior she had been more aware of what went on in Darrensberg when Francesca was still little more than a child.

'Look, Chessie,' she said kindly into the phone, after Francesca had ended her outpouring of words, 'don't forget that Dad and Dr Wilde were *always* rivals. It wasn't a one-sided thing by any means.'

'No, I do know that.'

'They enjoyed it at first, I think, thirty years ago. They used to send each other patients quite regularly, then have these elaborate showdowns at the Wayans Falls Golf Club. It was only later that it got nasty. Dad was way too self-righteous about old Dr Wilde's slightly old-fashioned ways, but I know James Wilde wasn't above spreading a rumour or two himself. He used to say that *I'd* ''come to a bad end''. I thought that was hilarious! Took it as quite a compliment, actually, at sixteen.'

'Oh, I would have too,' Francesca agreed, and they both laughed.

'Somehow, though, when Luke went through that rebellious phase the rumours got nastier and began to stick. Dad was at fault there but, again, it happened gradually, and it was Mrs Mayberry putting two and two together to make five that created some of the worst stories.'

'Like the ones about Dr Wilde drinking?'

'He fancied himself as a wine connoisseur at one stage, I believe, but I think it was more talk than drinking.'

'And the story of the woman in the shack and the post-partum haemorrhage?'

'You'd never heard that before?'

'I was fifteen, and butter wouldn't melt in my mouth, Louise.'

'Yes, you little darling. The youngest gets all the breaks!'

'Not necessarily,' Francesca challenged darkly.

'I bet Mrs Mayberry is still telling those stories, too, isn't she?'

'Actually, she is,' Francesca agreed slowly. 'I think she's sincere about it. She believes she's acting for the best.'

'And of course Dad does, too, you know, misguided though that seems.'

'But it's looking as if Luke Wilde's practice may not survive the onslaught.'

'Poor Luke,' Louise said. 'He was always a pretty great guy, actually. If I hadn't been *far* too old for him back then—gee, a whole four years older, it seems like nothing now, of course—I'd have *paid* for a ride with him on the back of that Harley!'

'I should call you more often now that I'm up here again,' Francesca said, considerably cheered by the conversation. 'And I should come up when I get some time.'

'You should! Montreal's only a few hours from you.'

'Only the practice is so swamped at the moment. I'm not used to it yet.'

'And if I didn't have six uncivilised kids, five of whom are not yet in their teens, I'd come down to you,' Louise countered cheerfully.

'Then we'll just have to meet up in Florida at Christmas, as usual,' Francesca said.

Thank goodness for cheerful, sensible Louise!

CHAPTER SEVEN

IT WAS over a week now, since Luke had stormed so coldly from Francesca's house, and she hadn't spoken to or even seen him since then. No—correction. She *had* seen him, from the corner of her eye, twice, as she drove up State Street, working on his porch in the long, light evenings of early summer. Her insides had immediately roiled with wanting him, and with the sick awareness of how her disbelief at his words must have quenched his own fire for her.

And then to have it proved to her so soon afterwards that he was right, that her father was so much to blame.

'I need to apologise,' she told herself on Wednesday evening. 'It won't do anything for our personal relationship. I doubt anything can resurrect that now! But I want him to know that if his practice *does* fail it won't be because of me. I'll write to him. It's the best way. I can't risk just calling him up and saying it and getting the words all wrong.'

As she ate a quick meal the right words—lots of fluent and elegant phrases—filled her mind, but when she'd disposed of the throwaway plastic meal tray and actually got down to the task all literary ability immediately deserted her. She sat in the study in front of the computer for fifteen minutes but couldn't think of the right opening so she moved restlessly to the kitchen, then out to the porch and then back to the study again.

Typing it *was* best, wasn't it? Keeping it to that professional level? Yes, definitely. Most definitely! At last fluency returned and she produced a neat, crisp page, courteous and apologetic yet restrained and rather formal. Then, when it had spewed silently from the laser printer, she took it out to the porch again to read it through.

It was a sultry night, with low cloud, steamy air and the threat of a late storm in the forecast. She sat on the steps, hugging her knees through her linen skirt as she'd done on summer evenings as a teenager, letting the air clear her head and watching cars go by. Watching for Luke himself, of course, if she was honest.

Tonight there wasn't much traffic. This end of State Street was quieter since they'd put in that one-way section further down. She looked down at her neat sheet of paper, having just finished her read-through—yes, it was good, it said the right things, it took the right tone—when there came the roar of a motorcycle down the street and she looked up automatically, thrown back fifteen years in time to when this might have been Luke's bike and her heart would be hammering at the thought of seeing him go past.

It *was* Luke's bike. She recognised the distinctive low-slung contours of a Harley-Davidson, and the black helmet he had always worn. There were other Harleys, though, and other black helmets. Was it really Luke? He'd never mentioned that he still had the bike. She looked. He was almost past. It had to be Luke.

She stood up, craning her neck, then ran down the steps so that she'd see which way he went. She was in time to see him leaning into the curve as he made a right onto Northview, which led out of town to the south-west. It *was* him, she was sure of it.

So sure that she quickly signed her name to the letter she had written, put it in an envelope and hurried up to his place. Silence. No one was in evidence. Just a single light on somewhere in the back of the house. Tiptoeing onto the wide new expanse of porch, she tucked the letter into the crack of the door.

There! That was the end of it now. Last week's kiss was as ghostly on her lips as that first one fifteen years ago now was, and last week's passion between them seemed like a weird dream. It was ended.

Luke found the letter after his ride. Hand-written envelope. Typed contents. The signature…?

Chess.

And it was an apology. Polite, professional, sincere. His guts twisted with regret as he read it. The things he'd said to her that night! And he'd had no real reason to accuse her of being involved. As she had said then, she had consistently given him the benefit of the doubt.

He paced the house restlessly, listening to the old floorboards creak beneath his feet.

Why had he been so hostile, he wondered, ever since he'd heard she was coming back? Was it jealousy at the fact that she was walking into such a well-set-up practice?

God, he was more of a man than that, wasn't he? It wasn't that, it was—

Fifteen years ago. It dated back that far. The night Frank Brady had confronted him in that nice, leather-filled study and said to him, 'I know what started the other night between you two. And it's stopping now, do you understand me? She doesn't want it. She's too young, she's got a future and you're… Well, what are you?' A despising glance had swept down, then back up. 'So, if I ever find out, if she ever comes to me and tells me you've meddled with her again…'

The threat remained unfinished, but Frank Brady possessed real authority in those days, and Luke hadn't taken the words as idle ones. Nor was he immune to Dr Brady's very strongly phrased suggestion that he leave Darrensberg.

Not that the scene alone would have been enough to put him off. But he realised with gut-wrenching, angry disappointment that Chess must have asked him to do it. How else could Frank Brady have known that they'd kissed? Hell, he'd been so damned nervous about doing it that he'd checked the windows to see that no one was watching! She must have told her father and asked him to warn him, Luke, off. Couldn't even tell him herself. He hadn't thought she was so weak. Just Daddy's little girl.

He left town only a week or two afterwards, with the dim realisation that there was nothing for him here—nothing at all, now that Chess had proved so fickle.

Then fifteen years passed—full years, with more than their share of tragedy, hard work and coming to terms with life. After the first few months he didn't think much about Chess. He wasn't the type to obsess impotently. When there was action to take he took it, but how could you act on what was only an odd sort of disappointment, combined with unslaked desire to form a nagging regret, like a piece of lumpy scar tissue beneath the skin?

Seeing her a few weeks ago, though, not having realised she was due to start practising here quite so soon, all the anger, disappointment and desire had coalesced into that first blast of hostile resentment. She hadn't changed! Good little Princess Francesca, getting her daddy to do her dirty work, like warning off an unwanted male or leaving her well ahead of the game in her professional life by fair means or foul.

It was only her genuine confusion and her apparently genuine desire to create a professional rapport between them which had opened a chink in his armour, giving him pause in his dismissal of her and allowing him to want her again, even worse than he had at eighteen. Incredible, that!

He clenched his fists suddenly. So she was too scared of me at fifteen to turn me down to my face? She was young and sheltered then, and she admits it. She's changed. And I've got nothing to reproach her with now.

He decided with all his old stubbornness, If there's still a chance…a chance to feel her against my skin…then I'm going to take it!

*   *   *

Chess couldn't sleep.

Of course, because tonight she particularly wanted to.

'So typical,' she groaned as she rolled in bed for the fiftieth time and felt her white cotton nightdress twist against her skin.

Tomorrow Dixie's sister, Dora, was starting as her new secretary-receptionist, and Mrs Mayberry was being so sweetly heroic in her stated determination to 'get things off to a smooth start with my replacement' that Francesca felt certain the day would be a disaster and knew she needed to be completely on top of things herself.

Surprisingly, though, after her bad night, the day *wasn't* a disaster, and Francesca knew that she had a jewel in her employ when Dora Sullivan, née Andrews, said very sincerely to Mrs Mayberry within the first three minutes of their acquaintance, 'Did you embroider that blouse yourself? It's *gorgeous*!'

Now, why didn't *I* think to compliment her on all her hand-made clothes? Francesca wondered. Because they really are very pretty, and beautifully done, too.

Because I've always taken them for granted, I suppose. I've known her since I was five. Things have been so hectic I haven't had a chance to think through the psychology here. To protect Dad, Mom kept insisting that the whole set-up was perfectly in place and all I had to do was walk into it, but I should have realised it wasn't that easy. I've been at fault, here, too.

This new knowledge gave her the large dose of very necessary patience required to deal with Mrs Mayberry fussing over Dora's orientation all day, and she even received the news that Dora already understood the system of the pink and blue examination rooms perfectly, with cheerful equanimity.

The day had some nice moments with patients as well. A pregnant patient who had happily weathered the change from old Dr Brady to Preston Stock to Francesca herself was three days past her due date now and could deliver at any time, and that was an excitement for both of them. It would be Lauren Gioco's first child, and Francesca's first delivery—other than the emergency over Caron Baron's baby, which wasn't quite the same thing—at Wayans Falls Hospital's very pleasant maternity unit.

Also, an old couple who had been seeing her father since he began practice came together for their annual check-up, and seemed so contented and in tune with one another that Francesca had to ask, 'How long have you been married?'

They looked at each other, smiled and said in unison, 'Sixty-one years!'

'My goodness, you must have been babies!' She glanced down at their charts. 'Gosh, are you in your eighties now?'

'We are,' Opal Craig said. 'I was fourteen when we met, and he was seventeen. I never looked at another boy after that, although I know George looked at a few girls because it was another seven years before he asked me out properly!'

'Then I asked you to marry me within a week,' he retorted easily. 'So you don't have too much to complain about, do you?'

It was obviously a routine they'd been through many times before, and they certainly seemed to support the theory that happiness and health were linked as they were both in excellent physical condition for their age.

After the work day ended—a little later than usual, as Dora's initiation into the arcane ritual of checking and locking up the practice took some considerable time—Francesca drove up to Ulmstown, a very pretty little village on the way to Lake Placid, where there was a cluster of antique stores that stayed open late on summer evenings.

Thinking about Mrs Mayberry and her home-sewn and hand-embroidered clothes today, she'd had a wonderful idea for a parting gift to augment her father's very generous cheque. In the third of the antique stores she found it—a large rosewood sewing-box, in perfect condition, with in-laid patterns of pale woods and mother-of-pearl. It wasn't cheap, by any means, but it was just right, and Mrs Mayberry deserved it.

Francesca was so happy about having hit on the right gift, and so careful as she carried it out of the car when she reached home, that she didn't even register the presence of Luke Wilde, sitting on the swing in the back garden, until she was within feet of him.

She almost dropped the box, and even after the first shock had passed didn't trust her grip so set it down very carefully and shakily beneath the tree from which the swing was suspended.

'Got your letter last night,' he said.

'I'm so sorry, Luke, for—'

'I know. You said it in the letter.'

Then words didn't matter any more. She was in his arms, responding with savage hunger to the onslaught of his desire. His mouth closed over hers and his hands made a searing exploration of every part of her—thighs through linen-blend trousers, back and stomach and breasts through silk blouse.

Yes, she was wearing silk again—a fragile barrier of fabric that seemed scarcely there, so little did it dull the intensity of his touch.

'Can we go inside?' he muttered, after he had reduced her to a quivering jelly in just a few timeless minutes.

'Yes.'

'Upstairs?'

'*Yes.*'

Neither of them had any patience at all. 'Which room?' he demanded as he breasted the stairs.

'My room. No!' The bed was too small. 'The spare room.'

'Wh—?'

'Where Chris used to sleep.'

It had been redecorated, of course, and the pale, modest Victorian look might have provided an odd contrast to the uninhibited heat of their passion if either of them had had time to be aware of it.

They didn't.

He was chafing at her blouse, laughing and groaning at his own clumsiness, and after a moment she pushed his hands away and dealt with the buttons herself, threw the garment back off her shoulders and fumbled for the catch of her bra.

'No, stop, Chess,' he ground out. 'Let me look at you first!'

She froze, her spine tingling at the way his gaze burned on her. There was something…incredible about being watched with such desire. It fanned the flames of her own need so that her breathing quickened as she stood there and her jutting breasts in their soft covering of lace hardened instantly and seemed to strain forward.

He stepped towards her and whispered raggedly, 'Why are we rushing this? We have all night, and even that's not going to take away a tenth of my need for you.'

He reached out very slowly and ran the tip of his fore-finger from her neck to the deep cleft between her breasts, making her shudder. 'Oh, Chess…'

He lifted his hands to her shoulders and slid away the straps of her bra, then reached around and unfastened it for her while she still stood, unable to move, intensely aware of every nuance of his touch. He cupped her with aching gentleness, and stroked her nipples white-hot with the balls of his thumbs, sending jolts of sensation singing through every nerve until they reached the very core of her.

Then he bent forward and touched his mouth to hers to taste her kiss, before drifting slowly, sensuously lower to taste her breasts, each in turn, with exquisite delicacy. She gasped and arched upwards, trembling and eager for more of him, and reached out to pick at his lake-blue shirt in search of his skin, but he wouldn't let her.

'Stay! Stay!' he said. 'Not yet!'

And he took her hands and pressed them back against her sides, sliding his palms up along her arms and then across to brush her breasts almost as softly as a breath of wind. Next, she felt his fingers nudging at her waist and a moment later he was sliding down her linen trousers and lacy cotton briefs, lifting her out of them and slipping her heeled shoes off with a nudge of his foot. Then he bracketed her hips with his hands, cupping her rear and pulling her against him.

'This isn't fair,' she managed breathlessly. 'I'm bared to you now, and you're still clothed.'

And yet his rapt discovery of her body, undistracted by his own nakedness, delighted her and made the fire in her flare still more. To feel him wanting her like this, to be aware as never before of how female she was... Her breasts felt fuller, her hips more sinuous and her hair more flowing.

He was pressing her back to the bed now, still kissing and stroking her—tasting her with his tongue from breasts to hips to the creamy insides of her thighs and sending her into a trance of ecstasy. Only when she was sprawled on the bed, her hair spread around her, did he lift his shirt and pull it over his head, then step out of his shoes and his dark tailored pants—all in a matter of seconds.

Watching him, her vision blurred with desire, she found that he was as beautiful like this as she had always known he would be. His skin was a natural peachy olive, fine-pored and smooth except where dark hair made a rough, patterned scribble. His muscles were tight and smooth and rounded, strong enough to display his flagrant maleness yet not unattractively prominent. His waist was trim and hard but not overly narrow and his thighs—but for the moment she couldn't even look that far.

He was on the bed beside her now, lazily brushing the

backs of his hands across her breasts again and then up her chin to pull her mouth to his.

After this she had no room left in her mind for detail, and neither of them spoke any more of taking it slowly— of their being no rush. She didn't even *know*. Was this quick or slow? Had much time passed as he pulled her writhing hips against his, kissed the straining fullness of her breasts, covered her with his warm, urgent weight and brought both of them towards full release?

Was it thirty minutes? Or two hours? She barely registered the fact that he used protection, barely took her mouth from his skin as she reached down to throw the light summer quilt over them both, didn't think about it as being 'finished' when their movements at last stilled and they lay together because being tangled like this without movement was as much a part of it as the rest had been.

A few moments later, while she was still only drowsy herself, he was asleep and she smiled up at the room's high white ceiling, loving the feeling of having his head cradled on her shoulder. She could feel his hair softly tickling her neck, and his arm was flung across her so that his hand could still cup the weight of her breast even in sleep.

For herself she felt too utterly sated, too complete and contented to doze now, but if he slept for hours she wouldn't care because it was heaven just to lie with him like this.

I love him, she realised, her heart quite full. It's crazy. How can I say that after such a short time? But I just do. And it *isn't* a short time. I've felt it since I was fifteen, like that wife today who'd fallen in love with her husband at fourteen. And now to *feel* him… Her cheeks were wet with silent tears, and she knew that whatever happened she had to cherish this, the memory of this.

Then somehow, not thinking it would happen, she *did* sleep, and woke a little later to find him sitting there watching her.

'Hi,' he said.

'Hello. I didn't mean to do that.'

'Do what?'

'Go to sleep.'

'Whew!' he drawled. 'For a second I thought you meant what we did before we went to sleep.'

'Oh, no,' she assured him earnestly, '*That* I meant to do!' And I don't have a particle of regret.

'Hungry?'

'Actually, yes, and I can smell—Luke! Have you been downstairs?'

'You mean, have I been downstairs naked? The sunset's glowing on the kitchen windows. The local voyeurs would have had to be pretty keen.' He held out a steaming microwave meal. 'You seem to specialise in these.'

She made a face. 'I'll start cooking soon. I *sometimes* cook.'

'Handy to have them in stock, though, I have to admit, for certain occasions,' he said. 'I found some wine, too.'

He poured her a glass of rich red liquid and she sat up to take it from him, and to open her mouth for the forkful of noodles and veal with mushrooms that he was offering.

It was a wonderful way to eat, she soon decided. The light was going now so he switched on the low bedside lamp, which cast long dark shadows across the rumpled white bed. Neither of them bothered with clothes, and there was something very erotic about eating naked in bed with her new lover—her new love—sprawled beside her, his male shape contoured and highlighted by the golden glow of the lamp.

He was still watching her, too, in the same way he'd watched her as he'd taken off her clothes, with a mixture of hunger and wonder that made her aware of every movement she made—the way her thighs slipped together as she rolled and stretched into a sitting position, the way her breasts fell as she leaned to rest her wineglass on the bedside table. He'd drunk only a mouthful of it himself, and it struck her vaguely that for someone who'd had a reputation as a hard drinker in his late teens he certainly didn't drink much now.

When they finished eating it seemed quite inevitable that they should make love again, less urgently this time and more thoughtfully, finding time for words and a little teasing as well as hungry discovery.

'Oh, God, Chess,' he rasped as their passion intensified once again. 'I knew it would be good. I knew your body would burn me up, but I didn't think it would be like this.'

'I didn't think it *could* be like this,' she managed, and then he pulled her down on top of him so that her hips locked to his and her breasts were grazed against the fine dark tangle of hair that covered his broad, hard chest.

They didn't talk any more for nearly an hour.

This time he didn't seem in the least sleepy afterwards. 'Ready to get dressed again?' he asked her, pulling his body away. She wanted to reach out and pull it straight back.

'Why?'

'Because there's something I need to show you.'

'Yes?'

'You'll see. Put on something comfortable. Leggings and a T-shirt. I'll be back in a minute.'

He had already dragged on his own clothes—very roughly, not bothering to put on shoes or button his shirt at all. Now he loped out of the room and she picked up her crumpled blouse, her trousers and her wantonly strewn scraps of underwear and went along the corridor to her own room, where she came up with a plain white T-shirt, years old, and some navy cotton and Lycra leggings, not remotely knowing what he had in mind.

She put them on in a fog, then found that she had forgotten her bra and that the T-shirt was really too tight. Did it matter? She didn't care.

He was gone for some minutes, and when he returned

he wasn't wearing his doctor clothes any more. He was wearing leather from top to toe—a heavy black jacket, black pants that zipped at the sides, and black biker's boots. He held out a large bag to her. 'There's gear in here for you.'

'What are we—?'

'We're going riding, if that's all right with you.'

'Yes. I think. It'll be a first, for me.'

He grinned. 'Thought so. That's going to be a treat for *me*, then, if you enjoy it. Those pants zip at the sides, like mine. The jacket might be a bit big.'

'Leather is compulsory?'

'Leather is compulsory. I don't feel safe otherwise.'

'Bikes are dangerous under any circumstances.'

'I know but, Chess, there has to be *some* danger in life!' He spread his hands. 'Doesn't there?'

She smiled uncertainly at him and couldn't answer, not yet sure if she believed this or not. It depended, perhaps, on what kind of danger you were talking about.

'Look, I'm pretty careful these days,' he added.

She couldn't help answering, 'Not *too* careful, Luke. I've always liked the danger in you.'

Their gazes caught, held, lingered on the parts of each other that were becoming familiar now. In his jacket his shoulders were bigger, and the shine of the leather emphasised the lean length of his thighs. The old T-shirt she wore offered little possibility of disguising the fact that her nipples had furled into dusky pink crests again, and she knew from his expression and from his hooded lids that he desired her once more.

Her hands shaking, she pulled the heavy jacket on and zipped it up, then took the pants and the boots he'd provided.

'Helmets are on the bike,' he said. 'And, by the way, you left your parcel outside. I brought it in.'

The expensive rosewood sewing box for Mrs Mayberry.

She was shocked at having forgotten it, but could only laugh. 'Oh, well… Luckily this isn't New York City. It's safe now.'

'Ready?' he said. 'Let's go.'

'I hadn't even realised until last night that you'd kept the bike, Luke.'

'Last night?'

'I saw you ride past.'

'Can't resist getting out on a summer evening sometimes.'

She assumed that this was all he meant to do tonight, that this was part of his gift to her—his body had been a gift, she felt—to have her experience a pleasure that was obviously very important to him. So this was how she approached the ride at first, listening very carefully to his instructions about fastening the helmet, finding the footrests, holding him and leaning into the turns the way he did. 'And no sudden moves, please.'

If I hate this, will I have failed a kind of test? she wondered.

But she didn't hate it. The night was a perfect temperature for this—mild as milk after another hot day, with thunder in the forecast again. No sign of it yet, though, and stars were visible overhead. When they began to move the breeze was immediately cool as it blew into the open neck of the jacket. His body sheltered her, upright and steady as she gripped his waist as he had told her to, and she loved her new right to touch him like this.

They went out along Northview and up into the folded, forested slopes that stretched for miles beyond the town, criss-crossed by a maze of back roads where city-dwellers' artfully rustic log cabins on the lake frontages contrasted with much smaller cabins and ugly mobile homes tucked away further from scenic attractions.

It was as they passed the second of these along a particularly isolated stretch of road that Francesca first had an inkling that this was more than just a pleasure ride. After several swooping bends and two or three turns at gravelly intersections, where the bike spat stones even when Luke slowed almost to a halt, they climbed a small, winding road and he stopped, idling the bike beside a rocky shoulder that was snowed thickly with pine needles.

He took off his helmet and she followed suit, shaking out the blonde hair that was pressed down untidily around her head.

'I used to ride up here all the time,' he said. 'I knew every road like the back of my hand. I was a bit crazy in those days—used to go too fast around these gravelly bends. Used to take off my helmet sometimes to feel the wind in my hair. Now *that's* nuts!'

'You've done your stint in the emergency room, right?' she guessed, knowing what those internship rotations usually did to any doctor's sense of their own mortality.

'Right,' he drawled in agreement. 'Back before then, I thought I'd live for ever.'

Their thoughts had taken the same track. At another time it might have seemed eerie. Tonight, though, with the connection between them…

'One night,' he went on, 'I was coming up this road. Just past the bend there's…well, you'll see it in a minute. The Baron place. Sharon had already moved out, and Mrs Baron had died a year or two earlier. There was the dad, and the other kids. The youngest, Tilly, must have been about seventeen.'

'Tilly?'

'Pastille. I knew her. She drank at the bars I…uh…used to go to then. She was kind of pretty. Not my type. Had a reputation, too. And I was at just this spot that night, going too fast, when I saw a shape on the ground. God, I only just missed it! And it was Tilly, crawling along in a trail of blood trying to get to the next place back down the road a quarter-mile.'

'Oh, Luke!'

'She was haemorrhaging. She'd tried to get rid of a baby but she'd left it too late, and whoever had helped her—that we never found out, because he or she had already cleared off—didn't know what they were doing. Her dad was in bed, and Caron had taken Daron to visit friends. Then, as now, the place had no phone.

'I didn't know what to do. I had no thought of going into medicine then, and was woefully ignorant of first aid. A deliberate blind spot, actually. I picked her up and laid her across the bike in front of me and managed to get up to the house, put her in bed. I tried lifting her hips, bringing her water, then hared down to town for Dad as fast as I'd ever taken those roads in my life.

'He called the ambulance, but it was a busy night and it took an hour to arrive. Meanwhile, of course, we came back up the quickest way we could. First and last time Dad was ever on my bike! But it was too late. There was nothing we could do. Sharon turned up in the middle of it and started screaming at us that we'd killed her sister.'

'She still believes that.'

'I know, and she refuses to listen to anything to the contrary. But Caron knows the truth. Those two have always taken opposite sides in everything.'

'You didn't need to show me this, Luke. I told you in my letter that I believe you.'

'I know. I guess it wasn't an easy letter for you to write either. I hated having to tell you what your father had done, to bruise your innocence—'

'Don't, Luke!' She wrapped her arms around him. They were still both straddled on the idling bike. It was an odd place to be having this talk, but right somehow. Nuzzling her soft cheek against his rougher one, she said in a low voice, 'Didn't tonight convince you that there's more to me than the sheltered fifteen-year-old you had a crush on? I've had to accept some things about my parents over the past week or so that weren't particularly pleasant, but I'm thirty now—my own woman. Don't, *please*, don't forget that.'

'OK,' he growled. 'Yes, your point about tonight is fairly convincing, I have to admit.'

They laughed and kissed briefly.

'I'm serious, though, Luke,' she pressed. 'You've inherited some bad baggage with your practice, but what I've inherited has its downside, too. Even now that he's chronically ill, my father wants any success I have to be completely on *his* terms. He wants to visit often enough to make sure I'm doing it all *properly*. He'll question any changes I make. I'm going to have to fight that, just as you're fighting the false story of what happened here that night and all the other stories that have sprung from it.'

'I wish I had your problems…'

'No, Luke,' she argued. 'I'm not saying it's a competition in hardship. Let's just realise that we have something in common, that's all.'

'Do you think we can make it work, Chess?' he asked on a low growl, and it wasn't absolutely clear that he meant their medical practices.

She answered him with that ambiguity fully in mind. 'I hope we can.'

'I…uh…thought we'd go in and visit Caron and baby Norad while we're up here,' he said after a moment.

'I'd like that.'

'Ready, then?'

Again she followed his lead and put her helmet back on, gripping his hard, warm waist again as he revved the bike and accelerated up the dark road. Having lost all track of time earlier, she suddenly realised it must be late. Ten? At least! But when she asked about it, shouting over the noise of the bike and the muddle of the helmet, he shouted back, 'Don't worry. They're night owls.'

A minute or two later he had propped the bike at the

front of the narrow, shabby and ill-placed mobile home and hung the two helmets on the handlebars.

'It looks better inside,' he told her.

A skinny and rather weatherbeaten man of about fifty opened the door for them and clapped Luke on the back at once, 'Hey, Doc!'

'Hello, Jim. In the neighbourhood and thought we'd pop in.'

'In the neighbourhood! That's funny. This isn't a *neighbourhood*.' This was a younger man with a pleasant but rather flat face, and Francesca realised he must be Daron, Caron's mildly retarded younger brother.

She and Luke had both stepped inside now. As he had indicated, the place was clean and tidy, although the furnishings were cheap and garish and the TV clearly the best-cherished object in the room. It was huge.

Caron herself beamed at the sight of them. She was sitting in an old vinyl lounging chair, feeding the baby from a bottle, and said defensively at once, after her greeting, 'I got scared with the breast-feeding, Dr Wilde. I didn't know if he was getting enough so I dropped it after a week and he took to this right away.'

'Well, breast-feeding isn't for everyone,' Luke returned calmly. 'He's looking good, Caron. Is your incision healing?'

'Still hurts like heck if I lift stuff... Guess I don't want Norad to put on weight *too* fast! But, hey, this is—'

'Yes, this is Dr Brady.'

'I'm responsible for that painful tummy of yours, I'm afraid,' Francesca said, above the blare of the loud TV.

Again Daron laughed, but when he stopped he gave a wince and held his right hand against his left one, which was, Francesca noticed now, heavily bandaged.

Luke had noticed it, too. 'Had a bit of an accident, Daron?'

'Oh, he cut himself in the kitchen, didn't you, Dar?'

Caron said quickly. 'Opening a tin can. Told you to be careful, didn't I, Dar?'

'Yes, you told me to be careful.' The man nodded obediently. He must have been in his middle thirties, a bit older than Luke. He was still holding his arm.

'That's a big bandage,' Luke commented.

'He likes 'em that way,' Jim growled.

'Yes,' Caron said. 'Thinks it'll make his boo-boo get better quicker.'

'*Your* boo-boo's getting better,' Daron pointed out.

'That's right, Dar,' his sister agreed.

'We'll just have a look at it, though, shall we?' Luke suggested.

There was a beat of odd silence before Caron said, 'Oh, you mean mine? Yes, sure, if you like. And the baby, too. Um, will there be a charge for this visit?'

'No, it's really a social call,' Luke assured her.

Daron thought this was funny, too.

But he was in pain, Francesca saw, and she was a little surprised that he was being so reticent about the fact. She'd have expected more of a child's frankness—tears even, if the wound was fresh and still throbbing. Admittedly, that bandage didn't *look* very fresh…

Caron's incision was healing nicely, her stitches removed and no sign of infection. The baby looked healthy, normal and contented, too. After he'd finished his feed and burped some of it back up, Luke checked his umbilical cord and his little circumcision, both of which Caron had been a bit worried about, but they were looking good, too, and fully healed.

'He's beautiful, Caron,' Luke told her sincerely. 'You're doing a great job.'

Caron smiled and thanked him but her attention was distracted, and Francesca saw that Daron was really moping now, not interested in the TV, not laughing any more at some of the things Luke said—quite deliberately, Francesca suspected—to tickle his ready but simple sense of humour.

'I want another tablet, Sissy,' he blurted, after clearly trying to hold the words in.

His sister frowned. 'You can have one when the doctors are gone, OK?'

'But it hurts *now*!'

'That cut,' she explained to Luke. 'He's a fuss-budget about pain. And he hates blood, don't you, Darry? Even the littlest bit of blood.'

'There's lots of blood come out of my arm,' he said.

Caron got up with a grunt of effort. 'Well, the doctors don't want to hear all about that, Darry. They want to get home. It's late! They don't sit up all night in front of the TV like we do.' She laughed, but it was forced.

Luke and Francesca edged towards the door, realising clearly that they were not wanted any more, and a minute later, after some fairly perfunctory goodnights on all sides, they were out by the bike in the cooling night air.

'It's a nice ride home,' Luke said. 'Downhill, and some great curves.' Then he frowned. 'But, hell, we're not going to do it yet because there's something weird about that hand of Daron's, and I'm not going to let it slide!'

CHAPTER EIGHT

'GUYS.' Luke knocked with brisk authority at the mobile home's door.

'Just a minute. Did you forget something?' Caron called back.

'I might have. Can you open up?'

'Just hang on a minute, Doc, would yer?' Jim said.

But Luke didn't hang on. There was no lock on the door so he simply opened it and strode in, with Francesca in his wake. They were both in time to hear Daron whimpering as Caron soothed him and unwrapped the last rounds of the untidy bandage.

'Hey!' Jim growled at the two doctors, his good humour gone.

Luke cut straight to the chase. 'What's the cover-up for, guys? What did Daron *really* do to his hand?'

The last length of bandage came away at this point and Francesca hissed at the sight of Daron's forearm. It was swollen and red, streaked with dried blood and choppy with small wounds.

'Ah, hell, he shot himself, that's all,' Jim admitted, clearly realising it was no use to try for any more secrecy.

'He was hunting wild turkey,' Caron supplied, 'so we wuz scared to take him to Wayans Falls in case they put the police onto him.'

Francesca knew, as Luke did, that turkey hunting at this time of year was illegal.

'This badly needs treatment,' Luke said.

'Yeah, we wuz thinking we'd have to go down in the morning if it wasn't looking better,' Jim said. 'There's got

143

to be bits of shot still in there, I reckon. I guess you'll report him now.'

'Did he get the turkey?' Luke asked.

Daron grumbled, 'No, I only got *me*!'

'Well, then, I don't see that I'd have to—'

'But I got one the other—'

'Shush, Darry,' Caron cut in, her tone a command. Daron shushed.

'I didn't hear any of that,' Luke growled. 'Did you, Dr Brady?'

'None of it,' she agreed soberly.

'But if I *do* hear any more reports of illegal shooting of wild turkey in this area…I'm fairly good friends with Officer McTierney, as it happens.'

'OK, Doc.'

'In any case, Jim, and Caron…' His tone was a command now. 'This guy shouldn't be handling a gun at all, now, should he?'

'He loves it, though,' Caron said.

'Not any more. I don't love it any more,' Daron was whimpering. 'I hate it now.'

'You know what, Daron?' Luke turned to him. 'I don't want to wait until tomorrow to do something about your arm. It's bothering you a lot, isn't it? And it looks nasty.'

'It hurts,' Daron agreed.

'We gave him stuff before for the pain,' Caron supplied. 'Guess it's all worn off now.'

'Jim, will you drive him down?' Luke said. 'I'll meet you at my office and we'll get it all fixed now, hey?'

'You be all right with the bub, Car?' Jim turned to the mother of his new child, his creased, lean face solicitous.

'Yeah.' She nodded. 'Just gonna fall asleep in front of TV, aren't we, Nor?'

'We'll expect you shortly after we get there, then,' Luke said.

'Want him to put the bandage back on?' Jim asked.

'Uh, no.'

The very thought made Francesca shudder. She was busy thinking about what they'd need to deal with it, and wondering if Luke had everything on hand. Wondering if he'd want her help, too. She hated the idea of being despatched home alone, after everything they'd shared earlier tonight, but Daron was Luke's patient, not hers.

The problem was solved before they set off. Back on his bike, he handed her the second helmet then said easily, 'I could do with your help, if that's OK with you.'

'I'd like to, Luke,' she said carefully, not wanting him to see how much it meant to her to have their professional as well as their personal hostility break down. 'I feel involved.'

He didn't say anything, just smiled, and she liked that, too.

The ride back down to Darrensberg was smooth and easy, and they had some minutes in which to set things up before Jim Muncie and Daron Baron arrived. They both exchanged leather jackets for clean blue scrub suits as well.

'If we find this is beyond us…' Francesca began. 'If any of those pieces of shot are too close to major blood vessels…' A rumble of thunder at that moment cast her words in a more ominous light.

'We'll have no choice but to send him to Wayans Falls,' Luke said. 'I want to avoid it if I can. Jim and Caron have scared him about the police, and he's not comfortable going too far from home. But we should be able to handle it.'

They did, although it took a while. Jim was asked if he wanted to be with Daron but he laughed ruefully and shook his head. 'I don't do too well with this sort of stuff.'

It was an ambiguous sort of answer that had Daron looking uneasy and starting to whimper again as Jim sloped out to sit in the waiting room. First they soaked the arm in a soapy antiseptic solution to clean the more superficial wounds as thoroughly as possible. Daron was apprehensive about even this, and Francesca wondered how he would handle the sight of a needle.

Not well, as it turned out. Luke had one diagnostic tool that Francesca lacked in her own practice—an X-ray machine, rather old but still quite adequate. They were able to locate two pieces of shot lodged in the arm, each well situated to permit its removal without complications. Local anaesthesia would definitely be needed, though.

Daron tried to hold his arm out and steady, but then the needle containing the local anaesthetic would approach in Luke's hand and he'd pull his arm away again.

'Don't look, Daron,' Francesca urged. 'Let's talk about something else.' But his flat, rather pleasant face was crumpling into tears now, and two or three more minutes of attempting to distract him only made him more agitated.

'I'll use some ethyl chloride,' Luke decided, then explained to Daron, 'We're going to make your arm numb with this spray so you won't even feel the needle when it goes in.' This tactic worked at last.

They still needed to distract him, though, because removing those two deeply embedded pieces of shot was tricky, especially with the limited set of instruments that Luke had on hand. 'A proper vascular set would be handy right now,' he commented, 'but there usually isn't a need for it so I haven't invested in one.'

Yet his touch was so sure, delicate and skilled, Francesca thought as she watched him at work, that the lack of more sophisticated tools didn't seem to matter in the end. Her own job was mainly to keep Daron from looking, but she stepped in towards the end to syringe in another antibiotic and soap solution in order to be quite sure that any foreign material had been removed.

Safely numbed to the pain, and with the worst of the probing over, Daron thought this squirting stuff was hilarious. Finally, Luke did some cosmetic work on the skin,

tidying the raw edges of the worst three wounds and su-
turing them closed, his hands again gentle and sure.

It was well after midnight by the time Daron was ready
to leave. He looked bleary-eyed and ready for bed, and Jim
had already fallen asleep, stretched out on the waiting-room
couch. They roused him and Luke gave him a short list of
instructions for looking after Daron—painkillers, antibiotics
and rest. An immediate call to the practice if any redness,
swelling or fever developed. A trip down to Darrensberg
again in two days' time so that Luke could check the pro-
gress of healing.

Jim Muncie's loud, rusty old car sputtered off into the
night a few minutes later, and Luke locked the side door.

'I'll walk you home, Chess,' he said.

'There's no need.'

'Hey! Let me. I'd rather have you in my bed, if I'm
honest, but you'd better be there at your place when Mrs
Mayberry arrives for work tomorrow.' He didn't need to
spell out why. 'Got your pager still?'

'Yes. Have to say I hope it doesn't go off. I've got my
first OB patient ready to pop any day now.'

They both heard another grumble of thunder as they set
off, sounding much closer now, and he took her hand.
'Let's not get wet. It's got colder now.'

It was too late. The rain had arrived, with only a few
warning drops before the full downpour descended. They'd
left their scrub suits on, though Luke had added his leather
pants on top again, and the cotton-polyester blend was
soaked in seconds. Both of them had dripping hair by the
time they ran up the steps onto Francesca's sheltered porch,
a little breathless and with their faces glistening with water
in the light that she'd switched on before she left.

'I'll leave you to it,' he said, about to dash back out into
the rain.

But she couldn't bear to have him go and reached out

and grabbed his slippery arm, saying, 'No!' He looked down at her hand, holding him.

'No?'

'No. Please. At least come in and get dry and borrow an umbrella. Or something.'

'That's all?'

'Only if you want it to be all,' she admitted in a low voice.

'I'd like a lot more.'

'I would, too.'

She unlocked the front door with rubber fingers and they tumbled inside. She thought immediately of the fire that was always kept set ready to light in her father's library to the right. Even in summer Adirondack nights could sometimes be cold. She went in there, found matches and lit it at once, only switching on the old Tiffany-style lamp which did not pool its narrow circle of light beyond the edges of the desk.

'What's this, Chess?' He had followed her, and was watching the spreading licks of flame.

'Aren't you cold?'

'No, but I'm glad you're lighting it, anyway, because the idea of peeling this scrub shirt off you and...' He didn't bother to finish.

He had reached for her wet scrub shirt and was lifting it slowly upwards. He whispered, 'Out on the porch, under the light, this was totally transparent, you know, and the way the cold and wet had tightened your gorgeous breasts... *If* you'd sent me back out into the night... I was trying to pretend that's what I was going to do, but...'

'You almost fooled me, too.'

The flames began to leap and he pleated the wet folds of the scrub shirt up under her arms, not bothering to remove it completely just yet, too impatient just to touch and caress her, it seemed.

She shuddered at the feel of his hands—warm, he must

have had them in his pockets as they ran through the rain—stroking and lifting her breasts, brushing each nipple with an achingly light touch before he did finally, and with great tenderness, pull the scrub shirt over her head.

She did the same to him, raking her nails caressingly across the hard contours of his muscles, and then they held each other in the firelight for ages, clad only in their drying scrub pants… Until those disappeared too and they fell to the thick Berber carpet and got lost in a tangle of timeless sensation and discovery.

It must have been about an hour later that they were awoken, and Francesca was at first so disoriented by the fact that she was lying naked on a rug in front of a dying fire that she couldn't even work out what that piping sound was until Luke said, struggling to sit, 'You're being paged.'

'OK.' She fought off the cobwebs of sleep and sated desire, and reached for the leather pants, which had her pager in a pocket. But when she looked at it there was no read-out of her answer service number on the small screen so that piping was coming from somewhere else.

'Well, hallelujah,' Luke drawled. 'Who'd believe it? It must be mine. That'll justify paying for the answer service for this month.'

It was the first sour note that had been struck between them all evening, and Francesca felt her stomach tighten as she watched him reach for his pager. Cold again now, she crawled closer to the fire, but it had died down so much that all she felt was a tepid glow on her back while the rest of her grew more chilled by the second.

'There's a phone in here on the desk,' she offered.

He nodded and picked it up to dial his service, and she couldn't help watching him and loving the sight of that magnificently nude male body—his back was turned to her—as he got the details of the call and asked some quick questions. Then he dialled the number he'd been given and after a scant second said decisively, 'Tom? This is Luke. How long has she been having the pains?'

Hearing this, Francesca didn't waste any more time. Noiselessly she let herself out of the room and went upstairs to dress, her chill disappearing as she teamed slate wool pants with a pale blue-grey angora sweater over a cotton blouse and dry underwear. Next she hunted up a shirt and sweater belonging to her father and hurried quickly down to Luke.

'Here,' she told him. 'I thought I'd better assume it was urgent.'

'Thanks.' Already wearing his almost-dry leather pants and boots, he took the garments she offered and slipped them on hastily. 'It is. My friend Tom's wife, Jackie. True labour, by the sound of it, and she's not due for six more weeks.'

'The twin boys?'

'Yes. There'd been no signs. I had her doing self-monitoring for contractions. She knew what to look for. I didn't have her on bed-rest.'

He frowned, as if doubting his judgement suddenly, and she bit her lip, not knowing whether to offer professional reassurance or not. As with so much in medicine, different doctors believed in different approaches. Some would have had any woman carrying twins on full bed-rest. Others, equally on top of the latest research, wouldn't.

She said instead, 'What's happening?'

'I'm going over. She's lying down. We may be able to stop it, but if not, and if birth looks imminent, I'll call an ambulance fitted for preemie transport, just in case. I don't want Tom driving down in this storm. He doesn't handle a crisis well. He ran off the road on the way to the hospital when their daughter was born. It was funny afterwards. He's still telling the story, but—'

'Luke…'

'Can you drive me home to get my gear? This rain…'

'I'll come. Let me. Why waste time? We can bring a full kit from here. I'm setting up to do home deliveries because it can happen out here, even if it's not planned.'

'I know. In winter, if the roads aren't cleared in time after a storm, things can take you by surprise.' Still he seemed to hesitate, then he added, 'OK. Why not? We'll use your stuff and go straight there.'

It was only a five-minute drive away, but by the time they'd got their gear in the car, braved the flooded streets and then run through the rain to Tom and Jackie Bailey's house her labour had progressed, and it didn't take much expertise to realise that nothing would stop it now. In fact, birth looked rather frighteningly close.

'Call the ambulance, Tom,' Luke told his old friend, who still 'fixed motorcycles', running a very successful garage and gas station in Darrensberg.

'She's not…? Are the babies…?' He was pale and shaky, and looked sick.

'It's going to be fine,' Luke soothed, gripping his shoulder, 'but we'll need to take the babies straight to hospital in a specially equipped ambulance, just because they'll be small. Look, I'll call. Francesca?'

'Yes.' She nodded. 'I'll get things set up.'

'Abby's asleep?' Luke asked Tom.

'Yes,' he said, calming a little at the mention of his daughter. 'I can't believe it, but she hasn't heard a thing. Not the thunder. Not this.'

'Then all you have to do is be with Jackie. Dr Brady and I can handle the rest.'

Tom gave a sudden sharp glance in Francesca's direction. 'This is Dr *Brady*?'

'Changed a bit, hasn't she?' Luke drawled, his long lashes sweeping down almost to his cheeks as he gave a slow, cat-like blink.

'It's not that, Luke. I thought you and she were at each

other's throats over— Oh, God, it's not important now, is it?'

Luke made the call down to Wayans Falls while Francesca went into the bathroom to wash her hands thoroughly, before examining Jackie Bailey between the contractions which were coming very close together now.

'Yes, you're well dilated,' she said. 'Seven centimetres, closer to eight, and your cervix is paper-thin, of course. These guys are going to be a handful if they're this impatient about life already!'

Mrs Bailey gave a shallow, anxious laugh. She was pretty and dark and, Francesca realised, had been a couple of years ahead of Francesca herself in high school. One of the cool, popular girls she'd never dared to even speak to then.

Their roles were very different now. 'Dr Brady, will it be OK, though?' Jackie Bailey begged. 'Where's Luke? Can the babies survive?'

'They can and they will,' Francesca promised, crossing her fingers that this certainty would be proven right. 'I'll check them with this special stethoscope now, and then I'll let Luke take over because I know you'd like that. Let's just have you rest and *try* to hold off on this birth for just a little while so that the ambulance can get here before they're born—OK?'

'Hold off?' Jackie moaned as a contraction came. 'You're joking, aren't you?'

'No, I'm not.'

It was touch and go. Francesca located both heartbeats and both sounded good, but the intensity and duration of the contractions now was a little scary. Those baby boys were much safer in their mother's womb for the next critical half-hour before the ambulance got here.

Luke was back now. He squeezed Jackie's hands between his and growled at her, 'Hang in there!' He looked a question at Francesca and she summarised what she had found. 'You're too efficient at this, that's the trouble!' Luke scolded his patient. 'You need to take *longer*!'

'Oh, you're cruel, Luke,' the labouring woman told him.

'Oops, she doesn't like my bedside manner, Tom.'

'I don't care if you have the bedside manners of a pig,' Tom retorted. 'Just let this be all right, OK?'

For twenty minutes the tension built with each contraction. Jackie's pain was becoming far more intense and they all knew that this was it when she announced, 'I'm feeling… I'm feeling as if I have to…'

And the ambulance wasn't here yet. There was no point in getting Mrs Bailey to hold back now, though. There was danger in it, in fact, because a twin coming six weeks early didn't need the added stress of a delayed journey through the birth canal.

Luke prepared himself to handle the delivery, while Francesca stood by to deal with the babies. Tom held his wife's hand and she pushed, groaning with effort, for all she was worth.

The first baby's head was born just as an enormous thunderclap sounded, and hard on its heels came the wail of the ambulance siren.

'Oh, thank God!' Tom muttered, and Francesca echoed the heartfelt prayer inwardly. This meant a proper transport isolette, oxygen and monitoring equipment.

The child—Alex—was fully born now. He breathed well on his own at once and cried lustily as his mother held him briefly so it looked as if some of the ambulance equipment might not even be needed.

Things moved fast. Francesca suctioned the baby a second time and checked him, placing him in the warmed isolette which had appeared almost magically. Luke had left the front door propped open, it turned out, quite heedless of the rain driving in onto the hall carpeting.

'He's doing well, Jackie. *Really* well!' she told the panting, tearful mother across the room.

But then Luke cruised over, his casual air not quite genuine and said quietly to Francesca, 'Next one, though is breech. I've never delivered a breech baby vaginally before. Have you?' From his tone, he could have been asking if she'd ever been to Disney World, but he wasn't.

'I have. Once,' she said. 'And I've watched it a couple of times, but…' Summoning all her confidence and her competence she went on, 'It shouldn't be a problem, Luke. The cervix will be stretched, and you can keep it open with your fingers and put some pressure on the fundus to bring the baby further down. We have forceps for the head or, if the baby isn't in distress, you can try a—'

'*You* can try. The honour is going to be all yours, Francesca,' he drawled, cutting her off.

'It is?'

'There's no room for ego here,' he stated decisively. 'We're going to go purely with expertise and, in this area, that's *yours*.'

She didn't argue. She didn't dare. And, besides, beyond a degree of adrenalin that came as Jackie moaned and panted through a contraction of renewed intensity, she felt a surge of warmth at the fact that Luke trusted her this much now—that the professional co-operation she'd wanted between them all along was happening, even if only in an emergency.

While Tom hung over his new son, now safely in the hands of the same ambulance officers who had helped with Caron Baron's delivery two and a half weeks ago, Francesca gathered herself. Luke was on hand. He had told Jackie what the situation was, and she seemed to be handling it without panic. Her task would be tougher this time.

They had the equipment so that wouldn't be a problem. A quick listen with the stethoscope showed that the baby—smaller than the other one, she thought, but pushed aside any useless worry on that score—was still in good condition. Feeling him, she found that he was a frank breech—the most common kind, and the one she'd both seen done and done herself. That was a bonus.

Reaching in, she timed her action with another contraction and manually eased the cervix open, pressing on the top of the uterus as she did so. She didn't want to force it, just ease things along. Another contraction and major pushing from Jackie brought the buttocks down, but she was having a tough time of it and Francesca felt herself starting to sweat.

Don't let it take too long! she prayed.

The baby's back was facing forward, as it needed to be. That was good. Now the small, bony bottom was born, which meant she had to take advantage of the brief space between contractions to manoeuvre each leg, flex each knee and deliver each foot…

OK, the torso was now fully out, slipping easily after the tricky manoeuvring of the legs. Now if she could hook a little of the cord and guide it through so that it wasn't being pulled… Again, she met with success.

'Hang in there, Jackie,' she said. 'Pant through this next contraction… Tom, she really needs you now! Luke?'

He nodded, listening to the baby's heartbeat as Jackie frantically controlled her urge to push, then gave a thumbs-up sign. The heart was still beating well, which meant that with Jackie's co-operation she could try this hardest and most critical part without forceps. The contraction was easing. There was no more time to waste.

Francesca straddled the slippery blue torso over one forearm, then reached in and found the baby's mouth, put her middle finger in there and her index and ring finger against the tiny jaw on either side. With her other hand, she put her middle finger in the baby's nape to keep it flexed, and rested her other fingers on his shoulder. Another contraction was coming. 'OK, *push* now, Jackie! Push with everything you've got!'

Jackie was shaking and groaning so hard it was almost

a yell, but her hard work was producing results. With only the slightest downward traction, Francesca was able to deliver the head safely. 'You've done it, Jackie! Congratulations!'

Luke suctioned the second baby and he, too, began to breathe on his own, although it took a little longer. Francesca loved the way Luke managed it, coaxing that first breath with gentle stimulation that didn't let Tom or Jackie suspect the short period of doubt. His torso was turning pink already, and the healthy newborn colour was spreading outwards to his limbs, although he only looked about three and a half pounds. The other baby was definitely bigger—closer to four and a half pounds.

'They're both so beautiful,' Jackie was saying. 'My boys. Abby will go wild over them. What a surprise she'll get in the morning. Oh. I guess they won't be here.'

The ambulance officers were already preparing to whisk the babies off to the small neonatal intensive care unit in Wayans Falls Hospital for monitoring. From their size and condition, though, Francesca judged that it wouldn't be a long stay. She would accompany them in the ambulance, as, presumably, would Jackie.

'You won't be here either, Jackie,' Luke confirmed, as the second boy—Max—was placed in the isolette.

'Oh. Do I have to go down? Now that it's over? Couldn't you keep an eye on me here? I just want to rest and then get down to see them as soon as possible. Wouldn't they only allow me a twenty-four hour stay, anyway?'

It was all worked out over the next five minutes, while Francesca helped prepare the babies for their journey and Luke delivered and checked the placenta, repairing the tear that Jackie had sustained during the second delivery. Jackie would stay here under Luke's care. With fluids, rest and monitoring, she would then be able to go down to Wayans Falls this afternoon and would be booked into a special home near the hospital for parents of hospitalised children.

The ambulance was ready to leave now, and the journey was uneventful. The babies slept, their vital signs good and their oxygen saturation just as it should be with the assistance of oxygen hoods. At the hospital Francesca gave the babies over into the care of the NICU staff with a thorough run-down of their history, and explained that Mrs Bailey would be down later in the day. Then she got a taxi home.

The storm had passed now. It was after six in the morning and already quite light, and the wetness of the night's rain was like mist on the morning grass. She yawned, feeling very happy. There hadn't been much of an opportunity to say goodbye to Luke at the Baileys' house, but she had felt so close to him that she hadn't needed it. They'd worked so much as a team tonight, first on poor Daron's shot-peppered arm, and then to help bring about the wonderful outcome of the twins' birth.

In between those two dramas had come the very different drama of their love-making, which made her swell and tingle with remembrance.

There was no time for bed now. She'd had a bare hour's doze in Luke's arms, and she had a full day ahead after only the limited restorative treatment of breakfast coffee. Somehow, though, fatigue didn't seem like a problem at all this morning. Happiness, she found, gave you energy to burn.

CHAPTER NINE

TEARS sparkled in Betty Mayberry's eyes, and Dixie and Dora beamed as they watched her. 'But this must have cost...' she began.

'It doesn't matter what it cost. You deserve it,' Francesca told the elderly secretary. 'And there's a little something inside it from Dad, too.'

They were all at lunch—at the Gables, of course—a foursome of women, saying farewell to Mrs Mayberry on her last day, and the newly unwrapped rosewood sewing-box sat in front of the guest of honour. 'The Andrews Sisters,' as Francesca couldn't help thinking of them, were shrieking with admiration as they examined the sewing-box more closely, and then Dixie brought out her own gift—a set of compact discs containing several of Mrs Mayberry's favourite Broadway musicals.

Francesca yawned behind her hand. There was absolutely nothing she could do about it, although she recognised it as a grave social sin in this setting. She had briefly mentioned the medical dramas of last night to Dixie and Dora and Betty, but had glossed over Luke's role in her account to the retiring secretary.

This is a nice occasion, and the tension has certainly eased, but I'll be glad when she's gone, all the same, Francesca thought. It will herald a new start.

A new start with Luke, too... The yawn was replaced by an equally private smile.

Things got so giddy over lunch that they were all a little late back, and their first two patients, both older women, were standing outside the locked side door, wondering aloud about whether to leave. An explanation of the cir-

158

cumstances, however, soothed any irritation. The women had both been with the practice for some years, and knew Betty Mayberry well.

'What will you do, Betty?' one asked. 'I hadn't realised it was to be so soon.'

'Well, a little sooner than planned,' Mrs Mayberry said stoutly. 'But as for what I'll do—persuade Alan to retire to South Carolina if I can!'

'Really? My sister and her husband have a place there.'

The afternoon continued in this vein and so they ran late, of course, which meant that after Dixie and Dora had gone, and Mrs Mayberry had done her final, ritual locking-up and made a dithery, tearful and very sincerely warm farewell, Francesca—still teary herself, after quickly changing into a sleeveless denim overdress with a cherry-red T-shirt beneath—went through to the kitchen to make herself a glass of iced juice, and found Luke prowling around the back porch.

Her heart was fluttering as she opened the door to him.

'Couldn't decide if this was a professional or a personal visit,' he growled. 'I did want to thank you for helping last night…'

His hands were thrust into the pockets of old jeans, and a dark, striped shirt was open enough at the neck to reveal the tangle of hair that Francesca loved. He didn't move to come inside.

'Can it be both?' she suggested tentatively.

They'd made love three times yesterday. It was in the air between them, eloquent in the way they did *not* touch now, just looked or looked away. This was all very new. And daylight cast things differently from darkness.

'Both, sure,' he said, frowning. 'Which first, though?'

'Um, which is going to take longest?'

There was a beat of silence. 'The personal part, I hope,' he said, and then they both grinned, and it was all right. 'Feel like a drive?'

'On the bike?'

'No, not the bike. That's a ride, not a drive. Can't talk to you on the bike, or look at you.'

'But I can touch you,' she suggested creamily.

'Yes, and those soft arms of yours around my waist *don't* make it easy to concentrate!'

'Then the car is fine.'

'And if you'd like a swim bring your suit. I have towels in the back.'

He nodded towards his car, which she now saw was already parked behind her garage, so she grabbed her swimsuit, her pager and her phone, locked the house and they were off, driving for twenty minutes to reach tiny, private Trout Lake, where it turned out a friend of Luke's had a small, modern log cabin with big windows overlooking the water and the crescent of man-made beach.

He had a key to the house but they didn't even bother to go in, just went down to the sun-baked sand since no one else from the cluster of neighbouring summer houses was there and to have it all to themselves was too good a chance to pass up.

It was gorgeous today. Not humid at all, just an endless reach of blue sky with the odd big fluffy cloud cruising across it. The lake surface was still and smooth, and the only sounds came from the summer camp on the opposite shore about half a mile off—the shrieking exuberance of children in the water.

Aware of each other, but not needing yesterday's urgency, they each stripped down to their swimsuits and entered the fresh, clear water, not saying much—not saying anything that betrayed the state of things between them until he commented caressingly, 'Hot pink suits you.'

'And black suits you.'

At which point he waded over and took her in his arms and they kissed hungrily, knowing it couldn't go anywhere but content with just this because they had hours ahead yet.

He was a good swimmer, she discovered a few minutes later as he sped out to the floating wooden dock using a smooth, fast-paced crawl. If it was a race she was content to let him win it, and covered the distance herself at a leisurely breaststroke, taking his hand as he helped her climb up.

The dock was still in the sun, its silvery-grey planks warm. They lay there to bask off the water's chill, and she asked him lazily, 'Any report on the twins?'

'Yes, doing well. They'll be monitored pretty closely for several days, but if no problems develop they'll go home. Jackie's doing fine, too. Normal vitals, uterus contracting nicely, bleeding already tapering off and bladder function good, too. They set off for the hospital at about four. Abby couldn't wait.'

'That's great. I'm so glad it went well after the dramatic start.'

'It means, though, that after our little discussion on circumcision I won't get to do the honours. It'll be handled by one of the paediatricians attached to the hospital.'

'I expect you'll get over it,' she drawled.

'I expect I will.'

Suddenly she couldn't bear the fact that they weren't touching. She sat up and leaned over to him tentatively, wanting him but not knowing how to say it.

'Luke?' That one word was all that came out, husky, questioning, hesitant, but that was all it took.

He sat up too and reached for her—her hair first, to tuck the pale wet strands gently behind each ear. Then he eased closer and brushed his fingers around the wide scooped neckline of her simply cut pink one-piece suit, to touch her shoulders, her collar-bone, the soft slopes of her breasts and the dark cleft between them.

Only then did he kiss her, slowly and fully, cherishing her with each commanding touch of his mouth and each languorous probe of his tongue. She closed her eyes and felt the whole world seem to spin lazily, the heat of the sun and the heat of her own body impossible to distinguish separately. 'I wish I could just peel off your suit, slide into the water with you and hold you there. But I don't dare,' he muttered, 'because I know I'd lose control. Is it…too male of me to suggest that we go? Back to my place, and…'

'Please!' she agreed fervently.

Inside the private part of his house, which she'd never seen, she found things as she'd have expected—neat, a little cheap, needing repair in parts, with just the odd place where he'd found the opportunity in his hard-driven life to acquire something beautiful. Like the quilt on his bed, which was a hand-made antique in the Amish style, with plain fabrics, mostly dark, pieced to make a glorious pattern.

She had little time to admire the quilt, though, because he peeled it back at once and turned to her, grinning. 'When I like talking to you so much, *being* with you, why am I in such a hurry to do this, I wonder?'

'Perhaps we'd better find out,' she murmured, feeling the new warmth of mingled desire and self-consciousness in her face.

'Chess.' He came to her, and after that nothing was important but the perfect joining of their two bodies.

She would have stayed that way, too, except that he shifted rather soon, untangling his limbs from hers to reach out and turn the clock-radio by his bed to bring the time into view.

'You're always doing this, woman!' he growled. 'Threatening to put me off my schedule!'

'What schedule?' she murmured a little sleepily, stretching cat-like in the bed.

But he had already gone, after pulling on a pair of navy blue briefs, and seconds later she heard him clattering down the stairs. His departure left her bereft and, unwillingly, curious. The sleepy question reasserted itself in her mind—what schedule?

Surely he was coming back...

She didn't wait to find out but dressed hurriedly and went downstairs too. If he had... What? An appointment, or something? She at least wanted to say goodbye, before heading home.

He was in his office. She heard sounds coming from that direction and let herself through the connecting door between his professional rooms and the private part of the house. Still thinking vaguely of an appointment, she went quietly through the waiting room, not wanting to interrupt anything—and was just in time to see him remove the point of a sharp silver needle from his upper arm.

In the doorway she gasped, and he looked up at once to see the instinctive horror in her face. What had Mrs Mayberry said?

'I've seen him stick a needle in his veins.' Now *she* had seen him, too. The sight didn't make sense at all, and yet it was there before her very eyes.

He was as immobile as she was now, still clad only in those dark briefs. He stared at her, scowling, the needle still in his hand, and his words, which came soon, were angry and hollow. 'You don't trust me, do you?'

'Yes, I—'

'You don't. I can see it in your face, as if I were reading a book.'

'Tell me, Luke,' she pleaded desperately. 'Tell me the truth!'

'I'm not a junkie, Chess.' It was a weary explanation. 'I'm an insulin-dependent diabetic.'

Too late, following his gaze, she saw the half-full insulin bottle sitting on his desk.

He turned to dispose of the needle, and the lid of the sharps bin squeaked. She remembered the distinctive yet familiar sound from her very first time in this office, weeks ago now. That was why he had had to bolt food and juice in the midst of the crisis over Caron Baron's eclampsia—because he'd recently taken his insulin shot, timed before a scheduled snack or meal. That was why he'd said a couple of times in her hearing, 'I need to eat.' She'd interpreted it merely as male impatience with hunger.

It all made sense instantly, yet there had been just those few horrible seconds of doubt. Not long, but long enough to destroy everything.

She saw the bitter disappointment in his face and understood it completely, which didn't stop her from blurting, 'Why didn't you tell me?'

'I was going to. Tonight, probably. Kept waiting for just the right moment.'

'Why not sooner?'

'There is a certain wariness,' he drawled. 'There have been a couple of women who couldn't take it. My last relationship ended after she'd told me she didn't mind, then discovered that she did.'

'*I* can take it.'

He shrugged, as if it didn't matter whether she could or not.

'I can,' she insisted. 'I mean, I presume you have good control of it.'

'Very. I worked hard at it from the beginning, when I was nineteen, and I've had good control for years.'

'But, even if you don't, I'm a doctor. I'm not frightened of—'

'That's not the issue at the moment, Francesca,' he cut in ominously, 'and you know it. God, to see it in your face just now! Your very first instinct was to fall back on all the worst rumours! Luke has a needle in his arm so, of course, he's a junkie, like everyone says. And if you're wondering why I let that idea persist when I could scotch it by spreading the word about my diabetes—one, it's no one else's business and two, it would create more scepticism than it would cure. Some people don't trust illness in a doctor either. The truth will get out eventually, of course—slowly, I hope—and by then I dare to believe that people will be ready to take me on my own merits—which I kidded myself that you had done.'

'You have a right—*every* right—to be angry—' she began.

He cut in, 'No, not angry. Worse than that. Disappointed. The way I was fifteen years ago when you went running to your dad after I kissed you to get *him* to warn me off because *you* couldn't handle it.'

'Ran to Dad? I did *not* do that! I *never* did that!'

'No?'

'No!'

He shrugged again. It was a maddening gesture. How dared he use it to suggest that these accusations, flung like missiles back and forth, were immaterial?

'You're wrong, Luke,' she told him crisply. 'And if you don't believe me then we've both got reason to be angry and, yes, disappointed, haven't we? You're right. For a second back there I doubted you and fell back on all the rumours for an explanation of what I was seeing. That was very wrong of me. But it's obvious I'm not the only one to leap to conclusions. I'd have practically *died* back then before I'd have sullied our kiss by talking about it to *anyone*! Did you really—*do* you really—consider me so spineless and so far under my father's thumb?'

'I...'

'Perhaps we're both carrying too much baggage, Luke, for this relationship ever to be more than basic sex,' she finished in weary conclusion.

'It's beginning to look that way,' he growled, staring broodingly downwards.

'In which case, I'm bowing out because that's not good enough for me. When there are problems between people—issues of trust, questions about commitment—then sex doesn't solve anything.'

'No, it doesn't,' he agreed again.

'Which means there's nothing more to be said.' Brave words!

This time he gave no reply at all, and half a minute later she found herself walking tear-blinded down the back lane without a clue about how she was going to get Luke Wilde out of her system.

CHAPTER TEN

THAT night the baby Francesca had been waiting for all week finally decided to make its appearance.

The first-time parents, who ran a bed-and-breakfast lodge tucked away on Lake Piper, called conscientiously at just the right time. It was nine-thirty in the evening, and Lauren Gioco had had about five hours of mild but steady pains, which had now built to the point of discomfort and were five to eight minutes apart.

'Yes, why don't you come by and I'll examine you, then you can either go home for a few hours more or head down to the hospital,' Francesca said, relieved to have this distraction. 'Yes, do bring your hospital bag because it's likely you will be going down.'

Indeed, when she examined the rather excited mother-to-be—in the presence of the very solicitous father-to-be—she was a good four centimetres dilated, with the pains continuing to intensify.

The Giocos drove down, which then left Francesca restless and unable to focus on anything because she knew she'd be getting a call later tonight or in the early hours when delivery was getting close. Frustrating! She wished, with the sort of unjustly felt irritation that even the best doctors had to admit to sometimes, that Mrs Gioco could have had the consideration to be either so close—about six to seven centimetres—that Francesca herself would have had to leave for the hospital hot on their trail, or so far—about one to two centimetres—that she could have sent the couple home again and told them to head down in the morning.

At ten she went to bed—what else could she do? She

was then awoken at four from a deep sleep by a call from one of the nurses in the Wayans Falls Hospital maternity unit. 'She's getting close.'

'I'm on my way.'

Why am I feeling so particularly *down*, and as if I just wanted to anaesthetise myself with sleep for another twenty-four hours at least. Oh, that's right—Luke.

The Gioco baby—a healthy, beautiful girl, Carina Marie—was born at six that morning. She was three weeks old before Francesca saw or spoke to Luke again.

He called to ask if they'd be able to share the management of another patient, who had just come to him for a blood test to confirm her pregnancy.

'She's an insulin-dependent diabetic,' he said over the phone, his voice sounding gruffly professional, with no words wasted. He didn't refer to his own diabetes at all. Their painful flare-up over that issue—and others—might never have been.

'Another refugee from New York City,' he went on, 'so she was a little sceptical of our expertise. With your knowledge of obstetrics, though, and my extra experience with diabetes, we should be able to make everything go smoothly, don't you think?'

'Oh, yes.' Francesca cleared her throat, buying time.

Clearly his call was a signal that he was now ready, if she still was, to ignore personal rifts for the sake of professional advantages. *Was* she still ready?

Pride asserted itself, and she seethed inwardly as she thought, God, about the only thing I can get any satisfaction out of here is that at least I'll behave like a professional! That was my only goal with Luke at the beginning, and it would have been better for both of us if I'd stuck to it!

So she answered him firmly, 'Yes, that sounds good. We can consult by phone whenever we need to.' And let's hope it's not too often!

But what was he saying now? 'Just out of interest...'

'Yes?' Very neutral.

'This couple are friends with the Saltmans. Did you tell Eric Saltman to suggest that they come to me?'

'I didn't tell Eric Saltman anything,' she said, 'other than that I was pleased his Graves's disease seemed to be responding well to the drug treatment. But my new secretary is telling people that I'm not taking new patients for a month or two until I see how full my load is once things have fully settled down. Whether these New Yorkers of yours tried this practice first, or whether they went straight to you, I couldn't tell you.'

There! She was quite pleased with herself about how suitably formal she had made that sound. If he had given her any credit for it, though, she couldn't tell.

'Right,' was all he said. 'I'll be in touch about this new patient, then, and she will be too—to make an appointment for a proper prenatal in a few weeks' time.'

'OK, thanks, then,' she finished briskly, and put down the phone, only to lean forward again to the intercom to buzz Dora.

'Be right there,' came the chirpy voice.

Dora's jewel-like status glowed more brightly each day. Coffee appeared at the right time. There were no tears. And the pink and blue rooms were now both painted cream with a mulberry trim.

'Although I have a horrible feeling,' Dixie had said as she'd surveyed the finished result last Monday, 'that we'll be calling them the pink and blue rooms for the rest of our days.'

'Yes, Dr Brady?' Dora had appeared.

'Just out of interest…' It was only after Francesca said it that she realised Luke had used the same phrase. 'How many new patients have we been turning away lately?'

'Oh, not many. Just a couple this week. And a couple of tourists who decided to go to Wayans Falls. On the other hand, though…' Dora hesitated.

'Yes, Dora?'

'There have been several requests lately to send patient

files over to Dr Luke from people who used to go to old Dr James, then started coming to us and now want to switch back again.' She winced uncertainly. 'I mean, I haven't made a big deal of it. Should I have? I figured if we were turning people away, anyway…'

'No, no, that's perfectly all right,' Francesca said absently.

'Was that all?'

'Yes, that's all.'

'Because I think Dixie's just sent Mrs Barkin into the blue room and taken her vitals.'

'Thanks, Dora, I'll be right in to her.'

So people were starting to go back to the Wilde practice.

Well, good luck to Luke. He deserved it. She wasn't going to be bitter and petty enough to attempt to destroy the Wilde practice, as her father had so nearly done.

Because— Hell, because I love him, she realised anew. I want to see him succeed, not fail.

As the days passed it became clearer and clearer that succeed he would. Lyn Parker was still with him so evidently he *had* been able to pay her at the end of her first month, and now the news filtered through the grapevine that Betsy Schwab had been taken on as practice nurse. Francesca couldn't help glancing across at his house every time she drove past it, and she saw increasing evidence of his greater confidence in his future in Darrensberg.

The porch trim was fully repaired now, the garden was being tackled—by Luke himself, she suspected—and now there were two painters at work on the house, scraping and caulking the old boards and nailing in new ones where the old ones had rotted. Within a couple of weeks that white and forest-green colour scheme he had spoken of back in May would be a reality.

She began to hear new rumours, too.

'Did you know he was diabetic?' Dixie asked one day. Then, without waiting for an answer, she went on, 'Lyn

Parker told me. Maybe that's where the drug-taking ru-
mours sprang from. And even that stuff about Pastille
Baron—who can get to the truth of that? I'd trust Luke
Wilde a mile before I'd trust Sharon Baron half an inch!'

It was high summer now, the middle of July, and Louise
and her brood came down from Canada for a visit, provid-
ing a welcome distraction. Then they left again, and that
seemed to bring the prospect of fall and then the cold
mountain winter into position on the horizon of Francesca's
life.

It was silly to dread the winter. It was still a long way
off, really. And anyway, she liked winter, didn't she? With
the snow? she found herself thinking more than once. I'll
ski.

But winter was when you really needed family to give a
warm centre to your life, and Francesca was starting to feel
oddly bereft of this centre. Is this all there is? she wondered
far too often. I'm in practice now, and I'm successful, and
I love being back in these mountains, but...is this all there
is? Oh, *hell*! I just have to get over him!

To that end she began to accept dates—one with a maga-
zine journalist who was on vacation with the Saltmans and
had come in to her office with a bad gash from a fish
hook—and the other with the owner of the second good
restaurant in Darrensberg, Lorenzo's. Both evenings were
very pleasant and very forgettable, and neither man had
asked her out again—probably because she hadn't been
able to summon the enthusiasm that would have encour-
aged them to do so.

Meanwhile, she saw Luke's pregnant diabetic, Veronica
Little, for her prenatal, talked to Luke about her case and
about a couple of other patients and ran into him once at
the supermarket—he was buying pesto sauce, a child's
birthday card, and milk—and three times very briefly at
Wayans Falls Hospital, where he seemed to be on good
terms with almost everyone.

Added maturity, she found, gave you added ability to

read a person through the smallest of signs. Whereas at fifteen she had woven incredible fantasies about Luke out of something as insubstantial as his silhouette on that bike of his, now she drew far more accurate conclusions about the man he was from even less.

That supermarket encounter, for example. Pesto sauce—therefore his tastes in food had broadened considerably from the hamburger diet of a teenage boy. A card reading 'For a boy who's 5,'—therefore he was the kind of man who remembered family birthdays. And milk, which made her think of him downing a large bowl of breakfast cereal each morning as he read the paper.

Oh, it wasn't fair! Why was she doing this to herself? Trying to know him better, even when she barely saw him. Loving him, even when she was trying desperately to fan the flames of her anger. Aching for him, just aching for him, every night, with a hopelessness that was worse than anything she'd endured on his account as a teenager.

Then, in early August, on a Saturday afternoon, her pager sounded as she was sitting in the garden swing, reading a romantic thriller. It wasn't a hardship to interrupt the plot. Reading these days was more an emotional anaesthetic than anything else. She returned the call that had come in to her answer service, and found it was from the Reverend Peter Epperley, who had been to see her for an ingrown toenail three weeks earlier.

'There's a woman who seems to have…that is to say, I get the impression she has…er…passed out in my church,' he said politely, so politely that Francesca had trouble initially in treating the call with any urgency. 'I thought she was asleep at first, then I thought she was drunk. She may, in fact, be drunk—or simply very deeply asleep—but I can't rouse her or move her, as she has fallen down between the pews. I'm wondering if she could have had a reaction to medication or some such thing. Could you come?' he asked, even more politely.

'I'll certainly come,' she assured him, feeling as if she

was accepting an invitation to tea. 'But is there anything else you can tell me first? Is she breathing? Did you feel her pulse?'

'Yes, she is breathing, rather fast, actually. Her pulse seemed fast to me as well. There's a funny smell about her, too. Not quite like alcohol, but as if she'd been drinking one of those tropical cocktails or something. Fruity.'

Fruity. The classic description of the breath of someone in a diabetic coma. Francesca pricked up her ears. On the other hand, though, it was a word that a non-medical person might well use in other circumstances.

'The thing is,' the Reverend Epperley was saying, 'she's a rather large woman, somewhat overweight, and I'm sixty-five myself and not in quite perfect health. I'm not completely sure that the two of us will be able to manage her. I did have a slipped disc a few years ago.'

'I'm on my way, Reverend Epperley,' she interrupted him firmly, still not at all sure whether she was dealing with a serious crisis that required an ambulance and immediate hospitalisation or a slight mishap that didn't need a doctor at all.

She did, however, take a substantial collection of supplies with her, including an IV kit and drugs to cover several possibilities, and then set off for Trinity Episcopal Church, a three-minute drive away, still half expecting to find the whole thing a false alarm. It wasn't, though.

Francesca recognised Sharon Baron as soon as she saw her, lying face down in the space between the back of one pew and the seat of the next. Sharon had been in to see her several times since that first visit three months ago with a range of complaints that came directly from her poor lifestyle and eating habits, although she would not acknowledge this and wanted a quick fix from Francesca every time.

'Look, I've found a clue!' the Reverend Epperley was saying, producing some used bingo cards from Sharon's skirt pocket. 'She must have been at Saturday afternoon bingo down the road at St Peter and Paul. Could she have…er, fainted in excitement at winning? Or collapsed with too much—'

'Thanks, Reverend Epperley,' Francesca interrupted desperately, feeling bad. He was obviously keen to be of help. 'This woman is a patient of mine, and I think she's suffering from high blood sugar. Could you please be so good as to—' This politeness was contagious! 'Please call an ambulance at once, and then call—' she couldn't even say his name without feeling that it was burning her mouth '—Dr Wilde as well?'

She had alarmed the reverend now, she saw at once, as she squeezed awkwardly along the pew and tried to assess Sharon's condition. Yes, she was breathing rapidly, and a pulse in her neck was racing.

'Oh, dear!' Peter Epperley said. 'Then I should have been treating this all far more seriously!'

'You weren't to know,' she told him, and he hurried out through the vestry to the church office beyond to make the calls.

Luke arrived within five minutes, while Francesca and the Reverend Epperley were still struggling to get Sharon out from where she had fallen between the pews, too tightly wedged and twisted to allow Francesca the access she really needed.

'We can't keep on with this,' she was saying, more to herself than to the reverend. 'I'll just have to put in an IV where she is—in her foot because she's lying on both arms. That's going to be hopeless, too, because with her uncontrolled diabetes her circulation in her feet is terrible. And I'll stick her shoulder to test her blood glucose—'

'Can't move her?' The terse words, echoing in the small church, were her first sign that Luke was here.

'No, we can't,' she told him, fighting her awareness of him. Craning to see Sharon, he was standing so close! 'I was about to give up.'

'That's a terrible position.'

'I know, but she's obese.'

'With three of us now… These pews are fixed?'

'No, but terribly heavy to lift,' the Reverend Epperley said. 'Awkward, too.'

'Not as awkward as our patient.'

'But Luke, if we try to slide it…' Francesca pleaded. 'She's wedged in. We may hurt her.'

'We'll slide the next one out,' he pointed out. 'Then we can move the one she's actually wedged against further forward and roll her onto the floor.'

It worked, but it wasn't easy. As the Reverend Epperley had said, the sturdy old pews were rock-solid in their weight. Luke was the only one of them who could actually lift. Francesca and the frail minister had to slide, which made a horrible dull scraping sound all across the rather worn carpeting, until the pew was slanted lengthways into the aisle, only narrowly making the turn.

'OK, let's take this second one,' Luke said, and then they did manage to lift it for the crucial foot to allow Sharon Baron to be rolled forward onto the church floor, giving access to face and heart and the better veins of her arms.

Now they could both work more quickly. Francesca checked Sharon's vital signs again with more accuracy, and confirmed that she was in a coma state. Then she pricked the woman's finger with a special lancet and used a glucose meter to obtain a reading of her blood sugar, watching it steadily darken on the testing strip for a full three minutes. 'Sky high,' she told Luke. 'At least 800.'

He was putting in an IV, and nodded, without looking up. Sharon's obesity made a good vein hard to find. 'Thought it would be in that region,' he said. 'There's the ketone odour, isn't there? How's her heart rate?'

'Up.'

'You've got insulin?'

'Yes.'

'And her pH will be way too low, I'm sure, but we'll leave that until she's admitted.'

'I'll give her a bolus of regular insulin.'

'Yes, go ahead.'

Meanwhile, the Reverend Epperley was standing in the background, rubbing his hands together nervously. When they reached the point where there was nothing more they could do until the ambulance arrived he offered tentatively, 'I suppose it's lucky I happened to be here. I had a couple come in for some pre-marriage counselling, and then I thought it might be a good idea to air out the church a little before tomorrow's service. If I hadn't come in to open the windows I wouldn't have seen her. Would—would that have been fatal?'

'Yes, it would, Reverend Epperley,' Luke said. 'So, yes, your visit was well timed.'

'I think you're right that she was coming from bingo, too,' Francesca told the elderly man. 'She must have started feeling bad and come in here to rest. She must have been feeling weak and very thirsty.'

'Here's the ambulance,' Luke interrupted, having been listening out for it.

He hurried outside to direct it and a minute later the two ambulance officers had arrived in the church with their stretcher. Transporting Sharon wasn't easy but they managed it, then Francesca told Luke, trying to sound brisk but coming across to her own ears as merely prickly and defensive, 'She's my patient. You don't have to come.'

They were both standing by the rear door of the ambulance, which was ready to leave. This *wasn't* the time for her to feel the sudden surge of awareness that swamped her. During two blissful nights, however, she had lain in this man's arms, knowing that she loved him, and it would take a lot longer than two months for something like that to fade.

'I know I don't,' he was saying shortly, 'but I believe in seeing things through.'

Although not their own relationship, apparently. In that area, he'd baulked at the first hurdle.

As I did myself? she wondered miserably. Is there any

way I could have, or *should* have, pushed harder? Not that he'd have made that easy.

She couldn't look at him—just had to stare with blurred vision at her hand on the ambulance door. There was no point in feeling this bitter tinge. It didn't ease the hurt. She was almost relieved that he didn't even reply. Just as long as she could blink back these tears before he saw them.

Had he seen them? She didn't know. He leaped into the back of the vehicle, his thigh grazing her arm briefly, and she followed him.

Sharon Baron was a buffer between them for the whole journey, and their constant monitoring of her condition made any sort of confrontation thankfully impossible. It was miserable to have to be with him like this, though. Utterly miserable.

No, think of your patient. Be professional.

Sharon was still at risk for heart attack and respiratory failure, but it was already looking as if their emergency treatment had come in time. Ten minutes before they reached Wayans Falls she stirred and opened her eyes.

'Sharon? Sharon, hello! You're OK. Do you remember what happened?' Francesca said quickly, trying to bring the woman to greater awareness by holding eye contact with her as she spoke.

'No.'

'You're fine now. We're taking you to the hospital. Your blood sugar got too high and you collapsed, but you were found in time.'

'Mmm…'

'Can you tell us what day it is, Sharon?' Luke came in.

There was a weak smile. 'Bingo day. Saturday. I won forty dollars. Hey!' She suddenly struggled to sit, and had to be soothed back into her reclining position. 'It's *you*! Luke Wilde!'

'Dr Brady called me to help with emergency treatment,' he said.

She just watched him in silence for a long while, making

Francesca nervous. She should have anticipated this, should have refused to let Luke come. Sharon's condition was still serious. Any emotional upheaval now…

'Years since I've had a good look at you,' Sharon said. 'Guess you helped save my life—is that what you're saying?'

'Yes, he did,' Francesca said.

'Tilly was nuts over you. See why. And you used to ride by our place all the time. Round then she started getting secretive. Mom was dead. It was all up to me. Caron never did nothing for her behaviour. I couldn't have Tilly running round like a slut, but she did anyway. Wasn't hard to tell. And what could I do? *Were* you the father of her kid?'

'No,' Luke said very simply. 'I just liked riding those roads.'

Again she looked at him, her coarse face creased and her eyes searching. 'I guess I believe you. What would you have seen in Pastille, anyway? Then it must have been Harry Petty that knocked her up. She was nuts over him, too. So was I till he got sent up to Dannemora for armed robbery!' She cackled quietly. 'Funny, it doesn't matter any more. But I wanted him *bad* back then, and Pastille knew it, so when she said the kid was his I thought she was just trying to get to me. Hey, if I came to you for a consultation, could *you* do something for me dyer-beatus?'

'You're the only one who can do that, Sharon,' he answered.

'Eh? Oh, I know, you're going to tell me the same old stuff about weight and diet. Doctors! All the same! Pay 'em to cure you, and they tell you to do it yourself. But they still take your money…'

She lapsed into silence again, her breathing rapid, panting and laboured, and Francesca reached out to squeeze her hand. 'Don't talk any more now, Sharon. Just rest, OK?'

They reached the hospital a few minutes later. She was admitted through the emergency room, and would then be transferred up to the intensive care unit as a bed was available and her condition was still far from satisfactory.

Luke and Francesca were kept busy for some time, writing orders, relaying the patient history, including full details of today's drama, and discussing the hoped-for outcome, which, realistically, was simply that Sharon would have had enough of a scare to be a little more responsive to immediate attention from a diabetic nurse-educator.

'Compliance is the crucial issue here,' Francesca told the emergency room's chief resident. 'She needs insulin, and perhaps she can get started on it in hospital… She'll only be covered for a stay of a couple of days so let's have them get right to it—she may find it's less alarming than she had feared, and if it starts to produce results and has her feeling better…'

'We'll do what we can,' the chief resident said.

'I think that's about it from my end,' Francesca said, and the tall, energetic-looking man nodded.

'See you around.'

He nodded at Luke, too, although the latter hadn't said much for the past few minutes. This hadn't struck Francesca at the time but now, suddenly, she sensed that all was not quite right, and her sharp glance, at first motivated by a very personal awareness, soon became one of purely professional assessment.

He was sweating, shaky, pale.

She said quickly, 'Luke, are you having an insulin reaction?'

'Of course I'm not!' It was an irritable dismissal, in itself a common symptom of the condition he was denying.

'I think you are,' she persisted. 'Tell me, how long since you—?'

It was too late to ask questions. With a very graceful pivot and a fuzzy, belated grab for the corridor wall, he dropped to the floor.

CHAPTER ELEVEN

IT WASN'T a very serious collapse.

Some quickly administered glucose soon brought Luke round sufficiently for him to eat a small packet of cheese-flavoured crackers. These would provide the carbohydrate which metabolised more slowly into sugar, but lasted longer than the more dramatically acting glucose.

The sweating, shakiness, pallor and disorientation disappeared within minutes. The irritability, though…

'I'd better get to the cafeteria,' he pronounced in a short tone to Francesca when the bevy of hospital people who had immediately surrounded him a few minutes ago had disappeared again. 'I catered for a solid meal with my last shot. Went for a hike this morning, too. Guess I underestimated how much energy I burned, and then not getting to eat after all…' He frowned darkly.

Still concerned about his condition, Francesca said, 'I'll come, too.'

'Don't. Please.'

'Hey!' She tried to tease, although her heart was twisting. 'You're only supposed to be this grumpy *before* you get some sugar.'

'Cut it, Chess. I haven't had a reaction like that in…must be twelve years. I just don't have reactions like that!'

Which, she realised, was quite enough to dampen any desire for humour. 'That's not good, is it?' she said quietly. Was that why he looked so hunted? Why his brow was furrowed like that, and why his blue eyes smoked with angry pain? 'But couldn't you just consider it a fluke?'

'I don't have flukes,' he muttered. 'I have control. It's important to me… Vital, in my profession!'

'Luke—'

'Don't push it, Francesca.' His voice wasn't angry this time, just weary.

She conceded defeat. 'I'm going to say hello to a couple of patients, then,' she said, more calmly than she felt. 'If you're interested in sharing a taxi back meet me out front in half an hour.'

'Sure.' He nodded. 'But if I'm not there don't wait.'

'OK.'

It had sounded like a threat. He wouldn't be there. She was sure of it. So sure that when the visits to two patients didn't last as long as she'd expected because one of them was asleep she almost didn't wait the full half-hour.

He appeared after twenty-nine minutes.

'Forget the taxi,' he said, and, although he didn't look exactly happy, there seemed to be a weight gone from him now and a new, purposeful energy to him—perhaps because he'd eaten properly.

'Forget it?' she said, uncertainly.

'Yes. Ronnie Parsons from the ER is going up to Ulmstown and she'll give us a ride.'

Francesca got the impression that the very pretty dark-haired Ronnie might like to give Luke something more than just a lift home, but if he was aware of this he didn't let it show. In fact, he seemed rather keen for the half-hour journey to be over, and when Francesca got out at her place he immediately got out, too.

His thanks to Ronnie were sincere and not at all off-hand, but after the young nurse drove off again up the street he didn't give her a backward glance and he was still beside Francesca when she reached her front door.

She could only turn to him. She couldn't find the words to express anything at all. Two months ago they had parted in anger. They had both made accusations and assumptions, and she had meant it that night when she had said there was too much baggage between them. Since then, though, she had racked herself with wondering whether that had been wrong and whether, as well as baggage, they both carried with them a much stronger legacy from the past.

The air—those sizzling few inches that separated them—vibrated with it even now. They shared the knowledge that what had flared in both of them fifteen years ago had somehow, contrary to all logic, not died as it should have done but had matured into a dangerously adult passion—and it wasn't showing the slightest sign of going away.

If she was speechless, though, with the intensity of what she felt, *he* wasn't.

'Francesca, I refuse to accept what you said two months ago! I *refuse* to, and I'm going to fight it every step of the way!'

She had her key in the lock and froze that way until his hand came to close over hers, engulfing it with hard warmth as he took over the action. One strong shoulder nudged at the door and she almost fell inside, just ahead of the arm that came to bracket her hip. A brief kick from his foot slammed the door behind them.

He spun her around and brought her hard against his chest, his lips just inches from her face. 'I'll start with a statement of fact:—Doing without you is killing me. What happened today with my blood sugar level is purely the result of my being so wound up over *you*. Whenever I'm not working I'm so damned distracted. I try walking it off, riding it off, I forget the schedule and the checks that should be—and are—second nature to me now.

'It can't go on like this! I was wrong to react the way I did two months ago. So now we get to the apology—I'm sorry. God, it's such an inadequate word, isn't it? You had the weight of the whole town's prejudice pushing you to mistrust me, and I'm damned lucky you only gave in to that for those few moments. After what I'd wrongly assumed about you, I'm scarcely the one to cast the first stone.'

'You mean…'

'Thinking you'd gone to your father all those years ago. I should have realised at the time. He must have seen us. I looked up at the lighted windows upstairs, but he must have been downstairs in his study, with only that small Tiffany desk-lamp which you still use. I noticed that night two months ago how little light it casts beyond the desk itself. And, of course, he knew that warning me off would be far more successful if I thought it came from you so he worded his speech deliberately to create that impression.'

'Dad has—'

'I'm not blaming him. Not really.' Luke gave a twisted smile. 'I have the strong suspicion that if I ever have a daughter as beautiful as you, I'll be the heaviest father that ever was. I was a poor prospect in those days!'

'*I* didn't think so!'

'You were fifteen—the classic age for bad taste in boy-friends. No, I don't blame your dad. It's what fathers are supposed to do.'

'More honestly and openly, in my opinion. Dad has a lot to answer for!'

'Perhaps. And yet I *did* blame you when I thought it had come from you. Was that wrong?'

'If I'd really been that spineless I'd have deserved to lose you.' Her smile was a little twisted.

'But you didn't deserve it,' he insisted in a low voice. 'And we lost each other. It had to happen, I guess. *I* needed the time to grow up, even if you didn't.'

He had his shoulder shored against the door and he was leaning over her, tall and powerful, making it almost im-possible for her to hold to the tiny distance that separated them, yet she was totally caught up in their talk—this exchange of every revelation that was important, cut back to the essential bone of it.

'I told you that first day in my surgery that I'd fathered a premature baby that died,' he said now.

'Flung it at me, rather than told me,' she pointed out drily.

'Flung it at you,' he conceded. 'But I didn't tell you the details.'

'Tell me now,' she commanded quietly.

He nodded. 'It was after I left here. A girl in New Jersey—the second and last of the women I took up with purely to forget you. She was a very successful model for a while but, like some in that profession, she found the glamour and pressure had come too fast when she was too young and she started to develop a habit…'

'Heroin?'

'Yes, and crack cocaine, too. Fortunately I was never that stupid. She got pregnant on our first night together. We were on again, off again, with each other for six months. She was still managing to hold onto a couple of modelling contracts, and was away a lot. Meanwhile, something was going wrong.'

'Sounds that way.'

'No, I mean in me. My health. I ignored it, made excuses for it, told myself it couldn't possibly be anything serious. I didn't know enough about the symptoms to recognise it for what it was. I was getting thirsty to the point of madness, although I drank what seemed like gallons of water a day, I had no energy.'

'Your blood sugar was climbing.'

'Rocketing. Finally, one night I lost consciousness on the bike, with Jaye riding on the back. We were both pretty smashed up. I woke up to be given the news that I was diabetic, and she lost the baby, which—'

'The world didn't need another crack baby, Luke.'

'No. No, it didn't. And yet…'

'It was yours.'

'It was mine,' he agreed. 'And when I came out of hospital it was as if the whole world had shifted. I'd lost a child. Jaye had disappeared. I heard months later that she'd gone back to her home town and made a fresh start. When we last talked, several years ago now, she was happily married and working on a graphic arts degree. So in a sense that accident turned both our lives around. I had a chronic illness to come to grips with. I knew I had to stop my self-indulgent rebellion against my father and my torch-carrying over you and turn myself into the person I knew I could be.'

'And you did.'

'I did. It wasn't glamorous. Made me resent you, whenever I thought of you, for the fact that you had it so easy.'

'Easy?' She bristled. 'Is medicine ever easy, Luke? Really?'

'No,' he conceded, 'it isn't. And I wouldn't have felt that way if I hadn't believed—'

'That I'd got my father to warn you off because I was too prim and timid to handle the power of what you'd done to me that night.'

'Was it powerful, Chess?' he whispered, his mouth a teasing magnet that he wouldn't let her reach.

'Just a bit,' she teased back.

'As powerful as…this?'

His kiss lasted for a blissful eternity, probing deeply into the sweetness of her mouth, compelling a response from every nerve ending. Almost aching with need and happiness, she wound her arms around him and stretched up on her toes to nuzzle his face, tasting him, teasing him with her mouth and pressing herself against his full masculine length.

He shuddered and groaned, and she felt his hot breath as he tore his mouth from hers and buried his face in her hair.

'Listen,' he said, his hands roving over her with wilful abandon as he lifted his chin again to stare searchingly down at her with those impossibly blue eyes that she loved, 'at the risk of jumping the gun here, I'd like to make my position clear.'

'Y-yes?' She couldn't really believe it was going to be something disagreeable, although his tone was forbiddingly firm.

Studying his face quickly to read his mood, she saw the

light of love there, as well as a very definite glint of purpose.

'Point one.' He ticked off on his fingers. 'I believe husband and wife medical partnerships can and do work. Point two, I'd like children before I'm forty. Point three, if you'll take my name and make the appropriate change to the name of the practice I'll happily sell up my house and move in with you. Point four—which should have been point one, now that I think of it—Francesca Brady, I want you to marry me before you really do kill me, woman!'

'Uh, should I answer those points in the order in which they were raised?' she queried wickedly, her heart pounding and her head going giddy.

'Reverse order?' He cocked his head pleadingly to one side.

'Reverse order,' she conceded. 'Point four—an absolute categorical yes.'

Further speech was made impossible for some minutes, by which time he had to remind her about point three.

'I don't want to spring it on you like an ultimatum, my darling, but it makes sense, doesn't it?' he said seriously.

'Francesca Wilde,' she mused. 'Yeah, it works.'

'I actually meant the prac—'

'And the Darrensberg Family Practice Center, partners Wilde and Wilde.'

'I wouldn't suggest it if things weren't picking up for me every day in my own practice. By the time we actually formalise the arrangement I hope I'll be coming to it as an equal.'

'Luke, you're better than equal already. Anywhere but Darrensberg you'd never have gone through what you have here, and even here, as you said, you're turning the tide,' she told him seriously. 'People believe in you now, and as for me…'

'It's your faith in me that keeps me going, princess,' he drawled—and then ducked the well-aimed blow that threatened to reach his ear.

But they were both laughing. Those ghosts from the past didn't have the power to hurt them now. Some hours later she said to him thoughtfully, as she burrowed her chin into his naked shoulder, 'How much before forty do you want children, Luke?'

'Hmm? Oh, you mean... Point—two, was it?'

'Think so.'

'Well, let's see, say about thirty-five?'

'Uh, Luke...'

'Yes, Francesca?'

'You're already thirty-four.'

'I know,' he answered cheerfully, and rolled her into his arms once more.

MILLS & BOON®

G Elizabeth Gage

The Collection

A compelling read of three full-length novels by best-selling author of A Glimpse of Stocking

Intimate

Number One

A Stranger to Love

"...Gage is a writer of style and intelligence..."
—Chicago Tribune

On sale from 13th July 1998   Price £5.25

Available at most branches of WH Smith, John Menzies, Martins, Tesco, Asda, and Volume One

SPOT THE DIFFERENCE

Spot all ten differences between the two pictures featured below and you could win a year's supply of Mills & Boon® books—FREE! When you're finished, simply complete the coupon overleaf and send it to us by 31st December 1998. The first five correct entries will each win a year's subscription to the Mills & Boon series of their choice. What could be easier?

Please turn over for details of how to enter ⇨

F8C

HOW TO ENTER

Simply study the two pictures overleaf. They may at first glance appear the same but look closely and you should start to see the differences. There are ten to find in total, so circle them as you go on the second picture. Finally, fill in the coupon below and pop this page into an envelope and post it today. Don't forget you could win a year's supply of Mills & Boon® books—you don't even need to pay for a stamp!

Mills & Boon Spot the Difference Competition
FREEPOST CN81, Croydon, Surrey, CR9 3WZ
EIRE readers: (please affix stamp) PO Box 4546, Dublin 24.

Please tick the series you would like to receive if you
are one of the lucky winners

Presents™ ❑   Enchanted™ ❑   Medical Romance™ ❑
Historical Romance™ ❑   Temptation® ❑

Are you a Reader Service™ subscriber?   Yes ❑   No ❑

Ms/Mrs/Miss/Mr ....Initials ....
(BLOCK CAPITALS PLEASE)

Surname...

Address ....

....

....Postcode..........................

(I am over 18 years of age)   F8C

Closing date for entries is 31st December 1998.
One application per household. Competition open to residents of the UK
and Ireland only. You may be mailed with offers from other
reputable companies as a result of this application. If you would
prefer not to receive such offers, please tick this box. ❑

Mills & Boon is a registered trademark
owned by Harlequin Mills & Boon Limited.

MILLS & BOON®

Medical Romance™

COMING NEXT MONTH

HERO'S LEGACY by Margaret Barker

Jackie had never expected to feel like this again and it was great! She realised that she'd been living in the past and now Tom was going to help her face the future.

FORSAKING ALL OTHERS by Laura MacDonald

Book 3 of the Matchmaker quartet

Siobhan thought that David was gorgeous but a playboy. If he wanted her he'd have to prove he was serious—it was marriage or nothing!

TAKE ONE BACHELOR by Jennifer Taylor

Could this gorgeous woman really be his new assistant? But Matthew wasn't tempted, after all he'd just decided to steer clear of women, hadn't he?

A MATTER OF PRACTICE by Helen Shelton

Kids and Kisses...another heart-warming story

The birth of their son and their heavy work-load had put a lot of strain on Claire and Ben's marriage. Ben was sure they could work it out but could he convince Claire?

On sale from 13th July 1998

Available at most branches of WH Smith, John Menzies, Martins, Tesco, Volume One and Safeway

Penny Jordan

COLLECTOR'S EDITION

The *Penny Jordan Collector's Edition* is
a selection of her most popular stories,
published in beautifully designed volumes
for you to collect and cherish.

Available from Tesco, Asda, WH Smith, John Menzies,
Martins and all good paperback stockists, at £3.10 each -
or the special price of £2.80 if you use the coupon below.
On sale from 1st June 1998.

Valid only in the UK & Eire against purchases made in retail outlets and not in
conjunction with any Reader Service or other offer.

30ᵖ OFF
COUPON
VALID UNTIL: 31.8.1998

PENNY JORDAN COLLECTOR'S EDITION

To the Customer: This coupon can be used in part payment for a
copy of PENNY JORDAN COLLECTOR'S EDITION. Only one
coupon can be used against each copy purchased. Valid only in the
UK & Eire against purchases made in retail outlets and not in
conjunction with any Reader Service or other offer. Please do not
attempt to redeem this coupon against any other product as refusal
to accept may cause embarrassment and delay at the checkout.

To the Retailer: Harlequin Mills & Boon will redeem this coupon at
face value provided only that it has been taken in part payment for
any book in the PENNY JORDAN COLLECTOR'S EDITION. The
company reserves the right to refuse payment against misredeemed
coupons. Please submit coupons to: Harlequin Mills & Boon Ltd.
NCH Dept 730, Corby, Northants NN17 1NN.

9 904170 250306 >

0472 01316